The Secret World of Reality

Tonya Jamerson

INFINITY
PUBLISHING

ISBN 978-0-7414-8154-2

Printed in the United States of America

Published February 2013

INFINITY PUBLISHING
1094 New DeHaven Street, Suite 100
West Conshohocken, PA 19428-2713
Toll-free (877) BUY BOOK
Local Phone (610) 941-9999
Fax (610) 941-9959
Info@buybooksontheweb.com
www.buybooksontheweb.com

This book is dedicated to

Brian Zimmerman.

I could stand here and pass 100 days,

but it could never amount to a moment

I had with you.

Table of Contents

Preface .... *v*

A Vaporized Dream .... *ix*

Premonition *1*

The Signal *9*

The First Portal *49*

Ambush *63*

Crimson Karma *75*

The Second Portal *87*

Justifiable Deception *100*

Wrongfully Accused *107*

Life After The Earthly Life *116*

Hail To The Queen *126*

Dangling Disaster *131*

The Celebration *137*

The Hidden Portals *149*

The Deeper Picture *155*

A New Circumstance *172*

The Communion *178*

Preface

Karma, according to the teachings of Buddhism and Hinduism, is the totality of any person's actions in any one of the successive states of existence, thought of as determining his or her future.

Let's put this concept into play in the Western world by examining one of Newton's laws that says that for every action there is an equal and opposite reaction, implying that the karma a person creates can manifest itself in a multitude of realities.

Now when it comes back, it can sometimes be tricky to detect, but is always distinctly aligned with the debt that has been accumulated.

For instance, let's say that an accountant named Cindy, who calculates multi-million dollar corporate transactions, decides to take a hunch off the honeycomb and deducts two dollars from every transaction. And then she filters the money into a mutual savings account for her and her hubby. She thinks of this as just giving herself a healthy tip.

And as she snaps the silver buckle on her briefcase, she goes home knowing that she's cheating the company....but blinks her bright eyes and stares out the office window at the navy blue sky, remembering all the times she had left the building tired from her 16-hour workday. She was the only one who had been working overtime, while all the other seats on the floor sat empty. The only light shining through the entire level was the one burning from the 60 Watt bulb of her desk lamp.

Her request to upgrade to a whopping 100 Watt twinkle was kindly extinguished by Bill, the supervisor, who sits behind those dark, double doors in that black leather recliner. The place is decorated with expensive furniture, which somehow got factored into the corporate budget this year.

It somehow didn't leave her mind how he told her about the company cuts that were coming right around Christmas time. He coughed, clearing his cigar-ridden breath, reciting the jolly carol everyone loves to hear: "Sorry Cindy, Finance gave us a print-out of what we need to do this year, and the lights are gonna be the first thing to go. Gotta put the main ones out at 5:00 p.m., and the highest watt I'm allowed to give out is 60...ya know?"

It was so hot in the building that day. And to top it off, what first looked like fog tucked in the corners of the glass windows turned out to be smog! Finance also decided to wish everyone a Merry Christmas by turning off the heat and getting in The Spirit the old-fashioned way, flaming up the cherry stone fireplace. This way they could eliminate more budgeting issues by slashing the electric bill. But management had remembered a little bit too late that they had forgotten to clean out the chimney…so the trapped fire and smoke had brought the heat in the halls to 97 degrees. Swirls of hollow smoke had seeped into the office and the smell had settled into Cindy's lungs, and it took nearly two weeks to get air freshener to zap out that scent of ash that had orbited the office and knitted itself into the nylon curtains.

In the end, Cindy reflects back on her past experiences with the company and just taps her hand on her desk to the melody of a steady drum to keep the rhythm of her accelerating thoughts. She swivels 180 degrees to the left in her chair, and then turns it to the right as if she were searching for a stable point on her moral compass. But her ears aren't receptive to what is right or wrong right now. All positivity has been tuned out by the melody that she's created by steadily tapping on the desk. She pulls back her top drawer and combs her fingers against the rough, wooden interior, but her soothing stash of bubble gum is all gone. Sitting in its place is a load of monopoly loot, courtesy of her cashiering supervisor.

A while back, management also promised her a bonus on her next check for top performance. But plans somehow changed when she brought her bonus-free check into the meeting with the senior execs and they politely clapped as she entered, while giving her a cup of tea and a fancy envelope stuffed full of rainbow cash. This was a symbol to recognize her as the highest collector in the building, and then her supervisor slightly tipped his cup to toast her grand accomplishments. Her heart sank like an anchor in clay that day. She had already dedicated her invisible bonus toward her lagging car note. But that's not gonna happen now because the world takes green cash, not the play money that comes from a monopoly case.

By embezzling the cash from this company, Cindy knows she is indirectly hurting others, but she can't forget how her eyes hurt so badly upon squinting to see the graphs on the screen. The room was constantly dim, but a random e-mail pop-up brightened the reflection on her spectacles as the message politely suggested mandatory overtime at 4:58 p.m. She bit her knuckles in resentment…this week the schedule had promised that she'd get to leave at 5 p.m.

Cindy added this snapshot to the rest of the files in the front of her mind as she cut off the bendable book light that dangled from the top of her monitor.

Upon the recollection of past events, the choice is clear: Cindy ends up cheating the company, but tragedy is gonna strike as her secret nest egg grows large enough and hatches into a hefty down payment on a house for her and her fiancé. This is the very moment when she discovers that he's been cheating the whole time, and he rationalized his indiscretions as a withdrawal from the pool of loneliness. Although she broke down in tears in front of him, he can't help but reminisce how she spent so many hours scanning the number graphs, and then was too tired to even rub his back, or bring home half of a good-night kiss.

After Cindy pulled the invoice on her hubby's whorish actions, it appeared that the karma she'd racked up by consuming more than her fair share of the company's account tallied up in the end. As she slapped him, her engagement band left a crimson imprint on his blushing, rosy cheeks. But what's with all this anger? She got what she bargained for…right? But as the moon cycles her rooftop more than 100 times throughout the year, it dawns on her that dawn will derive the same verdict: A huge, empty house with companionship from Jack…Jack Daniels liquor that is! This form of karma definitely crushed her spirit…but how can karma be cancelled out when society as a whole has a list of debits and credits, which leaves us in the red? Furthermore, who will strike the whip, while the fearful flinch in pain?

And what about the generations that strive toward a new day, but are continuously haunted by their ancestors' karma? They are the innocent ones who had nothing to do with the consequences that uncurled from their forefathers' wrongdoings.

Will the innocent also be added to the balance sheet and held accountable for the sinful transactions committed by their forefathers?

A Vaporized Dream

The tank churns. Air barely escapes from the accordion-like hose, and the plastic sack hanging over the lady's hospital bed perspires profusely, dripping down, leaving a foggy puddle on the hospital floor. A lady named Glory lies in the bed as her shallow breathing quickly fades, along with the hope of a full-on recovery. The sound of sorrow clicks on, and then off again, as the respiratory pipe makes a melody throughout the melancholy room. The walls are gray. Doubt clogs every artery of hope that once occupied the 300 square-foot cell. The pages of Glory's memory begin to flip back and forth, sketching out clear memories that are better left untold.

But the negative mood delves much deeper than just a series of venomous memories that pulsates in the shadows of the ailing woman's mind. This mood of bitterness has woven itself into the white curtains that hang along the walls, blocking out any type of light that could shed a ray of certainty on what truly took place to brew a negative temperature in the atmosphere. Her son cradles himself while he sits next to the bed, fighting the creeping anxiety of losing his mother due to something that's not even her fault!

Suspended in time, the vapor of death swoops down from up north, encircling old Glory's shoulders. It then tugs at the itchy hairs inside her son's runny nose. Sadness clogs his sinuses from his brow line to the slippery slope right at the dip in the nose…and it feels almost like a sneeze that just won't come out. Scratching his head, he wiggles around in his chair, but there's no escaping the uncomfortable question that has already crept into the room.

The question is as sweet as the bitter taste of medicine that makes your lips lock and pucker, while pinching one's eyes wide shut.

With his back arched like a dreary water fountain, he pumps up all the emotional courage he can manage to muster at the youthful age of fourteen. His stagnant emotions steadily gain speed as he asks her, "Why?"

Ruffling back the covers with her dried up cuticles, she gives way for her blue eyes to pierce his perplexity. Although her skin is painted pale with a couple of splotches of yellow, her crescent eyes still testify of her true, rugged feelings.

She bats her eyelashes, first up, then down…up, then down, until her eyes get wet enough to stay open long enough for a conversation. Her boy needs to know.

Sappy strings dangle from the corners of her lips as her grin sourly uncurls. Yet she musters up enough muscle to reach out and touch his hand. She asks him, "Well baby…why would you ask why?"

She starts coughing again, and then goes further to demonstrate true desperation, while clinching her covers tightly and hacking up sticky, black hell from her hollowed chest. She spits the residue of despair into her tin cup. But it's not just one or two drops this time. A flow that is the color of night rushes out of her mouth. So she tumbles her hand over a black box of Kleenex, only to realize that she can't even grab one given her worsening condition right now. The last one is clinging to the box, so Glory yanks with all the might left in her right arm, but with frayed cuticles and fingernails like plastic, her attempt is simply that… a failed effort as she continues to cough up more spoiled blood.

Pulling his bony fingers from the pockets on his black leather jacket, he reaches over and grabs the tissue for his mama. And then proceeds to light a cigarette for her to puff on and numb up her nerves. Since the last seven days, her sea-colored eyes have turned to the color of navy blue, and have since boiled down into a smeared black. The black of the eye muddles with the snowy white, melting into three different tones that range from deep brown to the color of the sky when it's half after midnight.

Glory somehow finds enough strength to snatch that last cigarette from her baby's hand. She then pulls her head into her chest, really close, clamping her gums down on the filter, and then she simply starts huffin' away.

"Light it up," she snarls as the cigarette's end begins to extinguish. The boy tries to light it again, but there's too much moisture in the air to even get the lighter to properly ignite. Her eyes plead with her boy, *Baby please...pass me a blow.* And he presses down on the lighter a thousand times as if it were a faulty morphine button. Yet, in the end, he's powerless against the interfering humidity in the room.

Yet this seemingly feeble female finds a pebble worth of power somewhere right beneath her bellybutton to snatch away the lack-luster lighter from her boy's hand. She then ducks down below the covers where it's cool and a bit drier...ya know...somewhere you can actually strike up a light.

Through the thin covers, the faithful flame flickers, and as it illuminates her silhouette, it's clear that she's as skinny as a gremlin, yet powered by the potent love of nicotine! She shimmies her shoulders above the covers, huffing, then puffing and bringing herself back upright. While pushing the baby blue blanket down toward her waistline, she sighs, "Ahhhh," exhaling an eruption of what some would swear was white, cottony smoke.

Patting her chest, she casually continues, "Baby...now you had a question for me?"

While hanging his head, he weaves his fingers together, clinching them closely. He asks her why God would let something like this happen to her. Yet she tucks her chin close to her shoulder as shame shadows the side of her face because she secretly feels at fault for befriending her murderer and having to leave her son behind. But not knowing what else to do, she gives him a blank reply.

"Well why ask why…what's done is done. That guy's gone!"

The boy resentfully replies, "But what he did is still here. He gets to run off free! The virus isn't stopping his vitals yet. He was deceptive…he came into our home…night after night…constantly eating free food and everything. God should be punishing him, not you!"

Then the conversation begins to smolder as she confesses, "Every day after work, I came home alone. I cooked alone...I had to pull up all the weeds alone. I just got sick and tired of being alone, ya know!"

That solemn statement cleared the foggy frame of a distorted picture, giving way for the precise reason why. This is a reason that's been drained from the bitter taste of deceit and enriched with the salt of truth.

There is no question. Her former lover carried the stench of a grave. Yes, he had HIV. But maybe this was truly an accident. When Glory phoned him with the results, he swore he had no idea that he was positive. But the odor he carried didn't come from being outside all day while working as a grave digger. No…it went undetected as a miserable secret that spotted his veins.

The boy wipes his nose clean with his sleeve and looks at his Ma, dead in her eye, so he can take in her memory. And as he takes a mental picture of her, his heart continues to blister with the rot of regret. The biggest part of all the pain is that he hasn't forgiven himself yet.

Nobody could have ever known for a second that the man with the comforting smile had caught the three-letter curse that kills…the one there is no cure for. He deceptively painted himself as a substitute dad who picked the boy up from school in the daytime and helped his mom out with small chores around the house. The tears just stream down the boy's face because he is slowly realizing the fact that his mother is steadily slipping away into the brink of darkness!

She leans over and clutches her son's arm really tight. Her eyes search his soul for a desperate sign of forgiveness for letting an outside man steal what little life she has left in her lungs. It was not her fault, but then again she thinks that it kind of was. Nobody likes being sick, but her life was ended by embracing a cold-blooded killer…one who tucked her kid in before he climbed into bed with her and slowly crippled her veins. The boy needed a father, and she needed someone to help her out from time to time. She made a mistake by letting him in, and her suffering beat the boy up badly inside. The anger of fatherly betrayal nibbled through his very bones. She is coping with the calm of death, but she's leaving a scared boy parentless. This is a young man without much wisdom of how the world works…one who could use a good friend right now. The "step-dad" the boy embraced left a cold imprint on his soul as the guy severed his mother's life strings. And as she drifts back under the covers and her subtle movements firm up, she sorrowfully cradles herself into a fetal position, while a whisper of wind silently sweeps across the tile floor.

Though he deeply loved his mother, the pain of losing a partner was so great that he subconsciously developed a thick skin around his soul that left a slight inability for his emotions to fully attach as they should. To avoid the pain of a loss, he subconsciously kept very few people close to his heart throughout his life.

The grand deception of subtle detachment at times produced lonely emotions, but the distant pain of solitude somehow covered up the heaping shame he felt for failing to guard his own mother from a masked murderer. This guy would smoke out S'mores with them the last Saturday of every month in the backyard, and he appeared as a friend.

The boy unknowingly embraced her unfaithful killer who tossed around the baseball with him at Throop Park. This was the guy who said The Lord's Prayer with him as he crouched down at the bedside with the family right before nightfall. This was the guy who killed his mom, the one who proudly announced, "Here's my boy" in front of the teachers with the plaid-skirts at the PTA meetings. Those three words, "Here's my boy," seemed to dust off all the shame he had felt in the past as the other kids sat next to their dads, with matching father-son jerseys and all. As he was growing up, he never really had a dad…he was constantly alone at the little league games. His real dad was just too busy layin' low with either Jack Daniels liquor or Sam Adams…two faithful friends he always seemed to find time for. He remembers the time when he had begged his dad to come out to just one game, and his dad pinky swore…telling him that he'd pick him up after school and take him to the game. But he broke that promise too. He had drank too much and blacked out before the school bell rang. He ran outside in a gust of excitement to meet his dad, but like always, other parents were there to pick up their kids, but his dad's red pick-up truck was missing in action.

Now Mom is gone too, and Dad surely doesn't give a damn. And all the boy has to his name is a grand total of: four socks, a pair of untied sneakers, a black leather jacket, and the love that expired from the woman who left him crying at her bedside as she took in her final breath.

Present Day:

Age 20

CHAPTER One

Premonition

A crumpled final notice reads: SIXTEEN DAYS UNTIL EXPIRATION OF SERVICES.

The year is presently 2031, and the boy who was in the hospital, Michael, has now grown into a full man. He nervously swallows four Excedrin as he gulps down a swig of warm well water…the free water that doesn't bump up the water bill. Beads of perspiration run down the glass of H2O, as sweat beads stud his forehead. He nervously crumples the notice, and then chugs down the rest of what is left in the glass.

Wiping a wad of water beads from the corner of his mouth, he shuffles up the red velvet steps to take a nap. The house is partially running off well reserve right now and all he can think about is that the bill collectors want their money upfront. Cash is dwindling, and as Michael turns down the A/C to conserve money, all he can hope for is that this deal breaks through with the record label in time to pay everybody out.

Last weekend, Michael sold out a plaza full of 300 people just performing cover music from the 80s. It was incredible! Then about half of them bought his latest single, and the website has had so many hits that they needed to get a bigger server just to keep up with the incoming fan mail and orders. But with growth comes growing pains. All the money he's earned is going into ordering new discs to burn the music on, and it doesn't look like anything is going to be slowing down in the near future! His team is trying to get it so that fans start downloading the music online, but people usually buy from him in-person at the local clubs and get more excited if they leave with something tangible in their hands. So the music needs to be on a CD too.

Not to mention the fact that Michael just bought this two-story house through a private loan. But the green river of revenue is stagnant right now. Sure it's coming in the future, but bill collectors want their pay on the 1st day of every month. And as much as sales go up, it takes constant cash flow to keep on producing the music. We're talkin' studio time, composers, the whole nine yards.

Michael continues to make his way up the steps, and with his heart beating at the pace of an irregular drum, he passes by the crystal chandelier that he got for half price from Home Depot, and finds its reflective, illuminating rainbow colors to be brilliant. He wonders if it could sell on EBay right now. Hmm…maybe…but it's dead in the center of the heightened ceiling, and it would cost him more money to hire a couple of movers to take it down, which would take a chunk out of the sale. He hears the chimes from the chandelier sway through his ears. He's so damn nervous to find another path to make some money right now that he locks the melody in his memory, hoping to sync it with a keyboard rhythm and produce a new hit and sell it online. But that's gonna take too much time.

As he reaches the top of the stairwell, he stares at the bronze lion that's studded with sapphire eyes, and in his mind he thinks he should be able to feel a sense of accomplishment. He bought a prized possession that thousands of suitors would adore. But the feeling of emptiness regurgitates throughout his system, bubbling at the threshold of his throat. A broadening bank account doesn't bind the open wound of a bleeding man's broken heart because it shreds from the inside.

Sure…it's his fault that he's in a bit of a financial bind right now, but even despite his circumstance, he just feels kind of empty. Once in his room, he asks Julie, his special lady friend, if she's heard back from the coffee lounge yet. The place usually stays packed with people whether it's day or night, and if he books this job, he should be able to sell enough to at least put a partial payment down on the lawn care bill. Cradling the pillow, she looks up at him as her hair softly drapes her eyes. But she has to shake her head in response to his question. The place had to close down for remodeling last week. So he sits on his bed and hangs his head. Not knowing what else to do, she rubs his back letting him know that they'll make it through this somehow, and he softly grabs her hand while placing it gently on the bed.

"Why can't stuff just stay set…I mean when one thing takes off, it seems like another has to slow down, and I'm constantly playing catch up." As he finishes these words, his head falls into the cradle of her lap, and he pats his forehead dry with his tie, watching the ceiling fan spin around and around. His girlfriend breaks the silence and says, "But I forgot to tell you that this one lady named Dape called for you today…she said something about meeting with you tomorrow at 3pm. She said she got your CD and liked what she heard!"

His eyes blink in amazement. This is it. This is the break he's been waiting for all this time. Dape is the girl he sent a CD to in Boston. When he called, she said she'd take a listen to it as soon as possible, but he never heard back from her. It took two months, but she finally called him back. He hops up, kisses Julie's forehead and asks her for the cell phone. She pulls it from under the covers and he grabs it in a grip of desperation. He hits the down arrow through the call history at least 11 times until he finds the familiar area code, and then presses the green call button. His electric anticipation produces a stream of harmony throughout the room, and his mouth can barely keep up with his words as he sets up an appointment to meet with her over a cup of coffee.

Michael stands in utter shock of what just dropped his way. His heart races with a prerequisite of confidence. Right when you think your life is skiing around the grime of the toilet bowl, *whap!* It's clean-up time, and it looks like a payday is in damn clear sight! He slips his slender frame into the shower, and somehow the slightly chilled water doesn't agitate him this time. The anticipation of a better future allows him to block out small irritations as a rush of optimism shields him from the common hiccups of the day. And as he later dabs himself with a towel, he smiles at his own reflection in the mirror wondering what tomorrow's meeting will bring.

The next day, as his girlfriend picks a loose piece of lint off his shoulder, he opens the door and his buddy, Dale, honks the horn as he pulls into the driveway to pick him up. Disbelief of a dream come true sparkles throughout the atmosphere as they prepare to pull off together. Although the car stalls for a slight second, it quickly shifts back into gear. Dale pumps the gas pedal, and again the rusty engine refuses to rev up and their faces fall like turtles that have been flipped onto their backs. But then suddenly it's a go again and the two smile at each other, chuckling in relief.

Dale just can't stop laughing. He unwraps a pack of bubble gum, and then takes a piece and passes it over to Michael, saying, "Geez…I thought this was gonna be an easy ride…ya know…"

Michael laughs with him, and prays that the car makes it the rest of the way. Yet his mind is later put at ease at the stop sign as he daydreams of all the gorgeous girls they'll soon have and all the records they'll be begged to autograph. But above all else, he craves the cash! How wonderful it'll be to finally be able to pay the rest of those bills off.

But as quickly as he daydreams of a future unforeseen, a black, frosted figure, wrapped up in a pinstriped scarf, quickly interrupts this still shot of good fortune. She's running extremely fast, but almost appears to be caught up in slow motion from a distance. Her scarf slowly ripples through the air like a loose leaf of sheet music. Yet close up, the lining of her legs and arms scurries rapidly like a character in an anime book that somehow turned onto the last page into reality.

"Hey, did you see that?" asks Dale. Michael just nods up and down with his eyes wide open, almost caught up in a glance.

He tries to pin the figure's motion to something that he's seen before, but he can't. The tip of his tongue tries to make waves, but his mind fogs up and freezes in the moment.

The two guys sit there and watch the figure fade off into the distance. "What was that?" asks Dale. But Michael doesn't say anything. It looked like a woman passing in a hurry, but she moved through the wind like a windup doll. It was actually Dape, but they don't know that. Michael shrugs his shoulders. Dale hates to have a question, yet no basis for an answer, but as he looks down at his watch, he notices it's nearly three o'clock…time for the meeting.

Sipping on a straw, Michael jokingly says that it must be someone catching the bus in a hurry that moves like that. Dale then accompanies his theory with a half-hearted laugh as he looks out the window.

Though the question is still bouncing around in Michael's brain, he decides to let it go and focuses on the chance of a lifetime that's just minutes away.

As they drive by the oak trees and old Chicago's lakeshore, the water is unmistakably clear today, so clear that you can see the catfish swim in unison along the meadow front. Their scales peak above the skin of the water, meshing with the sun's midday skyline. It's funny. You can

sometimes forget the true beauty that's imbedded in nature, especially when enclosed in a mansion with thick curtains that soak up sunrays so you don't have to use the air conditioner as much. But then, when you choose to step outside of earthly worries, there always lies love, the love of the birds as they fly in a V-Shape in unison. Michael marvels at the clean air exhaled from the trees, allowing us to breathe freely on a daily basis. This positive outlook calms Michael from within as he and his buddy turn into the parking garage at the Navy Pier. The two exchange a brotherly hug as Dale wishes him luck.

Mike grabs his disc and heads inside. He has walked into Bubba Gump Shrimp at least a half dozen times to get the famous tropical shrimp platter, and as the fresh scent of coconut oil sways around the tip of his nose, he can't help but feel stronger today. As he approaches the lady's table, he marches closer to her, and she is seated by the corner facing the shoreline, just as she said she would be. Today the seafood is the last thing on his mind as he wrestles with his heart and tries to keep his anxious emotions at bay.

He steps onto the deck and nothing looks out of the ordinary. Couples hold hands as they talk with one another, and the local artist strokes his violin, while the percussionist softly shakes up the tip jar, providing the mimicking sound of rain to add to the ambience of the slightly wet, yet still sunshiny day.

He gets closer to the lady that's waving at him, beckoning for him to come forth and have a seat with her. He humbly tucks his CD in his bag and makes his way to the table as she introduces herself as Dape, and he asks her if she's already ordered yet. She nods, extending her hand to the ceramic coffee pot sitting on the table as she passes him a mini cup to join in. She pours it for him, and then lets him know that the cream and sugar are in the tiny silver kettles. He reaches over for them, but the sugar slips from his perspiring fingertips. He grabs his forehead and chuckles, and she laughs to lighten the mood, placing her hand on top of his.

She whispers, "Don't worry…it's already got a little bit of sweet to it." They smile at each other as she begins to flip through the pages of her notebook, asking him how he managed to make all of these songs that people just love. He's had more opening shows than any other cover artist in the region, but he still chooses to do local shows instead of moving to the east coast where some of the bigger gigs are. He lets her know that he hasn't ruled that out of the picture yet, but his fan base is mainly in Chicago, so there's more support here right now.

She nods, understandably, and then he gets a call, but decides to hit the silent button. Yet she insists that he answers, as she smiles, sipping from her coffee cup. He puts one finger up, and then makes his way into the gift shop area, but as he answers the call, he receives a dreadful reality. The officials tell him that Dale has been in a serious accident, and as he asks them for the corner streets for the hospital, he comes over and apologizes profusely to the lady, telling her that he needs to go to the county hospital immediately. When she asks him what's wrong, he simply panics, putting his phone in his pocket as he heads out the door. He tries to flag down a taxi, but they all seem to be taken since it's the 4th of July weekend. Dape calmly comes outside and asks him if she can be of some help right now, and his eyes bulge as he repeats that he needs to get to the hospital a.s.a.p. She replies, "Well traffic is tight right now, but I know another way." She tucks her hand in his and they take off toward the Metra train station. Not knowing what else to do, he stumbles over himself and follows her toward the underground burrow.

All the people calmly drift through the boardwalk, with train tickets in-hand, but Michael's mind is in constant shuffle like the time slots on the destination board. Deep worry clouds Dape's eyes as she empathizes with his pain right now. And it's so strange because they hardly know one another, but he's willing to take a chance and follow her on this shortcut to the hospital.

Dape pays the fare, and the steam screams from the train engine, while air gusts from the automatic doors. Her hair blows across her face as she hands Michael his ticket and they step onto the expressway together.

"I've never been on this train before," he remarks, and then Dape stands a little bit closer to him as everyone crowds the boxcar, packing together like a picket fence.

"Don't worry. We'll be there soon. It's only three stops away. The conductor is gonna lift his hand and announce the stop for St. Anthony's right before we get there."

Michael then tightens his grip on the handle as the train amps up with speed.

CHAPTER Two

The Signal

As they both step onto the tile of the hospital floor, Michael makes his way to the front desk, and the sound of his steps ricochets off the cream-colored walls like ping pong balls. He begins to talk to the nurse, gently touching her forearm, and she then glances at the chart and points him in the direction of the east wing where Dale resides. He tries to make it into the emergency room, but the doctors interrupt him, redirecting him toward the waiting circle. He gets the diagnosis: Not expected to live after midnight. They promise to keep him updated on Dale's debilitating condition as they calmly head toward the break room, letting the door bang behind them. Michael slumps down in his chair like a loose saxophone melody that has lost all its air. He turns to Dape, a woman he's known for no more than two hours, and gives her a look of displacement. Earlier today he was headed to what he thought would be a music deal of a lifetime. But now his mood equalizes into a vibe of nothingness as his best friend's life dangles in the balance beams. His moist eyes turn to her, requesting direction in this matter. So she puts her hand on his shoulder, and he reaches across his chest to cover her hand with his. His long sleeve falls down a bit, allowing Dape to see the tattoo of a pyramid right below his wrist with the pharaoh's eye directly above it.

She rubs it and asks, "Not to intrude, but I don't see too many people with this type of emblem. I don't mean to cross any boundaries, but I'm curious…do you by chance practice the teachings of Sacred Geometry?"

This ancient form of sorcery has been long tucked away in the corners of Michael's mind. He never really spoke to anyone about it except for Dale, the only person he had kept in contact with from his devilish childhood days. Actually, Dale was the one who introduced him to the pharaoh's magic many moons ago.

He ponders her question for a little bit, and then thinks hard before revealing this sensitive side of himself to a lady who he just barely met, one who could possibly hold the key to his future in the music industry as well. He lets Dape know that it was silly child's play…stuff you do like truth-or-dare in adolescence. But Dape digs a little bit deeper to help him peel through the layers of time. She asks him if he still believes in the magic's healing power, and he tells her that it's been ages since he's even tested it out. Dape lets him know that of course business is business and she doesn't want to misdirect the nature of their relationship, but she must say that she feels comfortable with him…comfortable enough to let him know that he's in the company of someone who understands the vow of silence that one takes when undergoing a pyramid ritual. She then pulls back her sleeve to display the matching pyramid on her forearm, and Michael's eyes broaden with intrigue. He glances to the wing where he knows Dale has a lot of tubes hooked into him. And in the crisp of silence, Dape opens up her briefcase and pulls out a bag of chips. The two share a snack as Michael's mind paints a dreary picture of how he might have to lose a man who's like a brother to him…the guy who was there to give him his first tips on how to ride a bike.

Michael unravels the ribbon of time in his mind that's filled with still shots of good memories with Dale, and then he strokes his head, wondering why it didn't dawn on them to check the brakes. The car was obviously having problems. Guilt steadily seeps into Michael's soul. He was so filled with excitement to get to that meeting that he didn't even bother to check out the car and make sure that the brakes were working. The car was giving all the signals that something was wrong, but still they didn't check it. And Michael can't help but think that this may have been a mistake that's costing Dale his very life! And although Mike doesn't know this, forces in the spirit realm have been trying to prevent this accident from happening for a very long time. Before the wreck, mechanics had dulled all their tools trying to repair the car when Dale had brought it up to the shop some time ago. Yet they somehow overlooked the faulty brake pads.

The truth is that Dale's guardian angels had been trying to stop this tragic chapter from playing out in Dale's life script, which is the very reason why the car had been constantly stalling. The window of time for this potential car accident was left unlocked for three weeks. Unaware of a lurking danger in the air, Dale just kept pushing through the car's unidentified mechanical failure so he could keep running errands for everybody else. Yet the ultimate collision occurred on the 15th day from the moment that the window in time had first cracked; therefore, the spirit of death was allotted a vacancy. But Dape explains to him that there is a way to fix the frayed future for his friend.

She comforts Michael, but a slew of tears still stream down the slopes of his face as he repeatedly asks her why. There is no response that could extinguish his soul right now, but Dape reminds him of the power of the past. She uses Google to search for a picture of the pyramid on her phone and comes up with a rainbow-striped triangle; it's lined with gold and sectioned off by numbers.

She also flips through pics that she took years ago with the high priest in the spiritualist church. She explains how she used to practice the principles of the pyramid, and as she grasps her crystal necklace, which is filled with blessed water, she again asks Michael if he still remembers how to invoke the healing power that could help save his friend Dale. He gently flutters his eyelids as he slowly confesses that he is familiar with the rituals associated with the triangle. But he insists that it's been years since he's even tried its magic on anybody. Meanwhile, Dape lightly drapes his wrist with her hand as she encourages him to dig into his past for a friend.

"Do you love him enough to try and save him, Michael?"

He pauses. Sure, he understands the healing power that radiates from the practice of Sacred Geometry, but still chooses to shy away from a half-hearted attempt to engage in a new age type of white magic. So Dape jumpstarts the session, and as she clutches her necklace and heat and sweat race down her neck, she recites the beginning sentence of a chant meant to heal the weary. She glances at her phone to view a picture of the pyramid she found on Google, intending to engrain a visual concept of the image in her mind, and then the temperature drops at least 10 degrees. This is the magnetic point where the mind marries the universe as the sheets of reality are pulled apart. And in this game, even if someone recites the prayer correctly, but skips a step on the pyramid board, one could easily open a dimension that has been destined to remain closed.

He confesses to her how he loves Dale like a brother, but knowing that Newton's Law holds true in the supernatural, as well as in the physical, he tells Dape that he couldn't live with himself if he were to cause a rift in the spiritual realm and possibly cripple his friend's soul into an even darker fate because when you use jaded magic to do good, you always run the risk of its effects backfiring. Besides, he has shown his loyalty by offering up his blood to Dale for a blood transfusion.

"But a blood offering is purely physical," Dape proclaims. She continues, "But you and I both know that the real power starts in the realm. Trust me Michael, this is how it's got to be done!"

Michael stares straight ahead, avoiding eye contact with the woman who came with a business deal, but all of a sudden ended up suggesting the undergoing of the highest form of magic known to man. He is shaky about engaging in its practice, but his mind can't help but go back to all the times when Dale had been there for him. Plus, the spiritual realm remedies a bad situation quickly, and the doctors would just be playing Russian roulette, testing out the waters to try and bring him through the night with extra bursts of blood.

He asks her how long this ritual will take, and Dape tells him that she works quickly…two hours at the max. So she sashays her little slim frame about three-quarters down the hallway and then looks into a vacant room. She pulls back the curtains, verifying that the coast is clear…no nurses or doctors are in the little 10 X 12 space. She beckons for Mike to come forth, and he slowly peels himself off the seat to meet her in this dark, cool place. Michael sits down on the spinning stool, his back is as stiff as a filing cabinet, while his eyes dart from the left to the right…wondering what's coming next. She invites him to remove his jacket and relax, and he follows her command. But in order to further subdue him, she pulls the cork out of her necklace and puts the crystal bottle under his nose so he can soak in the fumes of myrrh water and engage in the magnetized atmosphere. As his mind slips through reality, the doorway begins to move in a ripple effect as if it were submerged under 5 feet of water. His perception has become watery by taking in the charming fumes. Dape slowly waves her hand in front of his face, and the slow motion effect then takes place. As she moves her hand up and down, he visualizes the illusion of seven hands.

The effect is the same as if one were flipping through a motion-based comic book.

In a daze, he asks her why the sound in the room is so muffled. As she walks across the floor, her steel-tipped high-heels sound like distant horseshoes. The atmosphere is giving off a foamy effect, shaving distinction off every sound wave. Dape lets him know that it's okay, his mind is simply mellowing with the universe right now, and the senses are meshing with a new type of reality. During this phase, it is sometimes slippery to grasp a clear grip of the physical. He looks down at his hands on his lap, and they are almost magnified, but when he pulls them in close to his eyes, each finger is a normal size. The drastic change in visual motion causes his stomach to churn, but he sucks down his saliva and decides to just deal with it in order to help a dear friend.

She asks him for his hand, and he puts his palm on top of hers. Dape then pumps the squirt bottle a couple of times and fills the dip in her other hand with the crimson sanitizer sitting on the counter. As she flips his hand over, she taps on his fingers and they slowly spread apart. She doesn't have any pens, so she must make do! Dape dips her index finger in the goo and paints the pyramid on the palm of his hand, and then draws a mirror image of the shape on the steel tabletop. With a few more strokes, she draws two vertical lines inside the shape, and crosses the rest of the pyramid with multiple, horizontal stripes, while numbering the blocks off. She asks Michael if he could spare a dime, and he fumbles around in his pocket, wondering what she could ever need with a dime right now, but manages to come up with one. She then directs him to throw it on the table and see which square it lands on inside of the pyramid.

He does as she wishes and as he tosses it, the coin taps the metallic tabletop, but then winds up all the way at the end of the table, and then falls on the floor. It rolls right by her shoes, but then she stops it with the tip of her toe to grab it

with her fingernails. The energy in the room gets hot as she blows on the dime for good luck. She then flings it onto the homemade board game, and it bounces from block to block, and then falls on lucky No. 7. Dape and Michael intertwine their arms together to create a 7-point figure with the frame of their bodies. "Do you feel anything yet, Michael?"

"Not yet," he replies as he pinches one eye shut and peeks with the other. So Dape leads in with a prayer. The language she speaks in is not English, but it doesn't necessarily sound foreign either. It is almost harmonious...bringing back the memories when Michael was a brand new musician just trying to find the melodies that harmonize in the highest tone. As a result, Michael joins her by humming and feels a gust of wind whisper up his sleeve and exit through the bottom of his shirt. The colors in the room begin to drizzle, as his senses become one with the vast universe, and the scenery smears into a dreary setting until it's too hard to distinguish the objects in the room. But then Michael blinks his eyes and the background goes blank.

He stands in a blank field of nothingness, but then finds that a CD is almost glued onto a clear wall in front of him. It manifested itself from one-thousand black molecules, which collectively clumped themselves together out of thin air. The disc is suspended in a new type of time as if it were trapped in a form of clear jelly or something. Out of curiosity, he grabs the disc and to his surprise it's a copy of his very first CD. Yet when he flips it over, his most potent memories of life are listed in chronological order instead of a series of songs. The flipside reads:

Michael Porter's Life

1) First Crush
2) Team Tryouts
3) First Day of School

The list goes on, almost endlessly, and he chuckles at the thought that his life stages can be categorized with simple titles. The design on the cover is a string of lights, and this shows how every major stage of his life is represented by a bulb, which is suspended on a line of time. Although he thinks he is all alone right now, Dape walks out in a vanilla flavored dress, which is studded with florescent pearls. She creeps up behind him as he reminisces upon the past valleys of time in his life, and the ground trembles just a little bit. The clear floor beneath Michael allows him to view clips from his time on Earth; it's like an intermittent movie that's projecting on a surface right beneath the veil. From up high, the view of Earth is like the setting of an ant farm, which is on the brink of maturation, preserved in plastic wrapping, just waiting for the right person to press play on reality.

"Boo!" she jokes, and Michael turns around quickly, smiling her way, anxiously grabbing her hand to show her some of the pieces of his life, which have somehow been captured right beneath them in a stream of time. She then pulls the remote control from her pocket and asks him, "Now which part should we watch first?" He scratches his head, wondering if she created all this. As he lends a voice to his thoughts, Dape assures him that she is definitely not the master designer. But she is more like the coachman, who can show him all his necessary exits he'll need to take in order to truly unlock the power of his vision.

She double clicks on the plus sign on her remote, bringing the first still shot into magnified focus, and then asks him what's going on in this picture.

It plays out for roughly 10 seconds, and he tells her that it must've been the night that he played at the Hard Rock Hotel. At that time it was the biggest crowd he had ever seen before. He had to take down three glasses of gin and tonic just to loosen up his joints and inch toward the microphone that night. That's when the dark, velvet curtains went up, and witness the fact that the letters have sped up in motion with symbols between them this time. With his mouth wide open, he stumbles over himself in pure shock as he tries to grasp this equation. The light fades out, and in pure black, he feels like he is all alone right now. And as he swipes to grab onto Dape's arm, his fingers constantly rub against the rubbery fabric of a translucent type of time. Yet if one were to tune the ears to a higher frequency, you could hear it. As he rubs against time, it sounds almost like a scratching record, which is stuck on repeat mode. But Michael comes back with nothing…just fists full of hot air.

The sweat evaporates from his brow line, and Michael's eyes gloss as the humongous question mark spins around in his brain, scrambling the divided thoughts that have thickened in his mind. Indeed he does remember rolling out of a raunchy romp with a serious hangover the next day, but he would have never imagined in a million years the devastating, agonizing, everlasting dilemma that would soon ensue after a heated 20-minute session with a seemingly playful girl.

Stroking his fingers through his hair, he doesn't know which way to turn right now, nor does he see anyone to confide in except for the doctors who are suspended in the opposite side of reality and are oblivious to his omnipresence at this time. He tries to wipe the foggy glaze off the veil as it illuminates, separating him from the doctors' suite, but it doesn't wipe off at all. By touching it, he just gets more of the sticky jelly build-up on his fingers.

But in the distance, he hears a feint melody, almost like it's coming from a music box. So with the hope of finding someone else out here, he tries to brush the tears from his eyes and pace toward the soft sound. Though all traces of water evaporate quickly in this dimension, he keeps wiping his eyelids out of habit, just in case someone were to see him in such a broken state of being.

But the light, which shines brightly from the other side of the veil, illuminates a winding path. As he makes his way down an ebony trail that is barely paved, he winds around a small twist and sees a door that's slightly cracked with a beam of light bending beyond the entryway. He runs toward it, but with each step he takes toward the light's reflection on the floor, it seems to pull away in a dimming manner.

And the ebony pathway just trails off into a gem-studded tile in this section of the zone. See the walls are sectioned off, slab by slab, in a vertical fashion. They scale from 0-5, then from about 5.3 to 11. Sometimes the smaller numbers after the decimal break off like pieces of fallen glass because they're not in sync with the next level. They actually interlock with a separate, parallel portal, where solar wind gusts by your face and the stars get as close to your cheek as a lover's kiss. The smaller numbers after the decimal are generally not calculated into the specified equations on this floor.

For instance, in our world, if you take one step toward your relative north, then you've travelled roughly 3 feet across the floor. But in the realm of "The In-Between," the measurements flip a bit depending on your speed variance. And if one's molecular frequency registers with the section of the first scale and the individual is simultaneously stationed within the zone of a three, then the rules make it so a man can never reach a room that rests on the plane of a 7. But if you extend beyond the section of a 5 by passing the intermittent blast of light that comes after one passes a solid number, then you can automatically get transmitted into the velocity of a 5.3, where one can be in sync with the motion of the higher scale and successively reach a station that is allowed to link to the frequency of a 7.

Meanwhile, Michael was able to pass into the point where he is able to move closer to the glowing door and is instantly granted a sweater to shield him from the harsh temperature. The melody of the music box still lingers softly tries to vomit to make room for pity in his stomach, but the only thing that comes up is another clip across the movie screen, and he pleads for Dape to stop right now.

Feeling the type of sorrow that you'd feel for a newborn who was born with just one lung, Dape pulls her shawl off her shoulders, and on bended knee, cradles him with the cloth, triggering a sense of security. He needs to feel this right now. Endorphins slowly cloud his body, but the effects have trouble registering with his mind. But Dape's tears somehow shower serenity on this grim, darkened day.

"I love you, Michael," she says, while forming a warm wreath of trust between the two of them. While crying, he automatically feeds her the same words, saying, "I love you, too."

She goes on to explain, "But after the drug kicked in, you're collected clarity checked out, and you still needed something to level out your hormones that night. That's when you decided to partake in this young girl's body. Except this time, she had other plans in mind for you..."

Dape tries to rewind the movie clip to the second when the vixen mounted her prey, gently licking his neck, and running her fingernails through his long mane. He reached in his pocket, and then crouched over to strap on the condom, slowly leaning back to allow her to move in for the kill. And just like a mantis, she made her way toward him with her head ducked down and slipped her hand toward his private region to pleasure him some more, and then pulled off the plastic, protective seal, reclining him in the Lazy Boy. His mouth malted with liquor as the sound of the TV and the beautiful woman clouded all his reasoning.

Now once in pure contact with her victim, she bounces up and down with the thrust of a bull. Sweat rolling down her neck, she leans close to Michael, and he can't help but be mesmerized by her pretty eyes. They're so clear that he can see himself in her gaze as she throws her neck back in exhilaration. Their howls could have been heard in the distant skyline that night. And after climax, he drifts off for a nightly retreat.

The morning mist will bring the sad reality that another beautiful soul has been crushed and broken by the curse of the plague as unwelcomed guests fester in the rapid rivers of the veins, crippling the immune system, later destroying the dignity of being able to care for oneself.

It's a soured fate indeed, and as the movie clip winds down, Michael is able to visualize clear confirmation that he does indeed have HIV in the physical realm. He is engulfed in the spool of universal time right now, but it's almost like a plastic film is separating him from the earthly world as well. He is able to see through the veil as he watches the doctor lean against the medicine cabinet in the physical realm. The man strokes his fingers down his moustache, and then gives his counterpart a thumbs-down after glancing at Michael's HIV test results in order to complete the blood transfusion for Dale. Michael tries to reach out toward the 3-D reality, clinging to the life that he once lived, and it appears to be slipping away. But as he tries to break through the clear substance, his hand gets trapped in a translucent type of putty, which rejects his attempt to abruptly cross back into the physical plane. He turns around and pulls the remote out of Dape's hand, pleading with her to let him stop the tape at once. He jabs on the red button, and then the green one, and finally the one that's blue. But the scene of intimacy just keeps rolling on, almost mocking his misery.

Suddenly the lights go out and only the center spotlight remains on as a stream of microscopic sentences race in an intersection across his torso. He is marked with the beast…the curse that kills as it further encodes his DNA. The tiny crimson lettering is shadowed by a type of black fuzz, meant to make the message a bit bolder. Michael smudges his fingers all over his chest to get an idea of what's going on right now, and then he feels the tiny pieces of hair stand up on his neck. He tilts his head further down and can't help but he slightly choked on the smoke while putting out his joint as he sang the cover, "Every Rose Has Its Thorn."

Thirty minutes prior to his performance, the stage crew had told him that the sound system had got fried somehow, and they were gonna be without an amplifier for the night. So he had asked for all the velvet curtains to be lifted so the fabric wouldn't soak up so much sound. Yet the crowd still delighted in the acoustic version of the melody, and the honey-flavored sadness made almost everyone stop and think about the first time they lost that special someone. Yeah…that song was so good, it got all the girls going…especially one girl who insisted on being led backstage.

Dape pauses the film as she asks him, "What happened here?" Now shirtless in the clip, he shrugs his shoulders and blames what happened next on bodily chemistry and basic human attraction. He sees Dape fumble with the play button a bit and warns her that this movie is about to go from a G-Rating to Triple-X, and she tells him that she's a big girl and can handle it. As the picture continues to play out, Michael marches back toward the dressing room as his eyes are bloodshot red and he has a ribcage full of reefer. Still subdued from the influence of Lady Liquor, he runs his hands across the wooden slabs of the hallway walls to find his way, as his new lady friend holds him up to escort him into the dressing room. Unfastening her 5-inch boots, she bends over as her hair falls down to the ground, wiggling her hips. She slips off her stockings and boasts her chest in his face, gently guiding his fingers down toward the crease in her bosom.

The scene gets deeper and deeper. And on the other side of the screen, Michael informs Dape that she is free to leave the room at any moment, but she lets him know that it's okay as the clip unwinds further.

Then the point of intimacy appears on the screen, and Dape chooses to pause it at the very moment when the young lady decides to remove the rubber condom that Michael had fastened tightly for safety's sake. With his head tilted back and his belt buckle far from fastened; his eyes are filled with a haze of smoke. Michael just lies there defenseless against this woman's delectable deceit.

He hiccups as he watches her rub his back in the film and charm him with her kisses, exchanging Ecstasy from her tongue to his lips. She brushes her hair back and saddles his slightly conscious body like a lone star ranger, pinning him to the pillows, making sure he can't shake free from this web of pleasure. The scene continues to unravel and Dape takes a break from the mini movie, asking Michael what he's gathered so far.

"She had a hot body, but not a huge conscience," he replies, while looking at the screen.

Dape's weary eyes look at the floor, and then modestly make their way up Michael's slim frame. She sifts through thoughts of the finest etiquette, but still can't fathom a softer way to tell him this dream-shattering news.

Sorrow fogs Dape's pupils, and she explains to him, "Now Michael, years ago that girl visited you, but she wasn't alone." He then assures her that no one else came backstage with him that night, but Dape reminds him of the carnal rule, which states that Satan attaches himself to people and it was horrible that he met up with her. Michael tells her that if the girl got pregnant or anything, then he'll pay his fair share of child support, but Dape shakes her head to let him know that she had given him a virus that cannot be cured.

The sap of sorrow silences his mouth, stopping him from muttering another word. He ponders this thought and pleads with the heavens, hoping that it's not the three-letter curse, but Dape nods slowly, and he thinks he's gonna be sick. He runs to the left, but it's just another sea of enclosed white nothingness. He wallows in fear as he falls to his knees, wondering how he could've fallen victim to HIV. His temperature hits rock bottom and his bones feel like ice. He in the air. Yet it plays at an extremely high-pitched tone in this zone...much more than it did when he was walking within the slower speed limit. But at least he kind of knows where he's going at this point. He opens the door and to his amazement, Dape is sitting there with her legs crossed with a white shawl draped over her lap. She waves at him kindly, but Michael is still a little bit confused. She just abandoned a serious situation back there! The lights went out and he didn't even know where to go at that point. And she sits there like nothing is wrong with an angelic smile painted on her face.

He asks, "Uh, Dape...what's going on...where'd you go?" He dashes to his knees and calmly touches her arm, asking, "Am I dying now?"

She drops her head into her book and lets him know that she didn't mean to leave him at that crucial time...that's simply not her character. But he needed to advance to a new level on his own during the growth spurt. This is abstract, but it's still a part of the game that allows the subject to unlock the elements that lead to internal strength.

And in regards to his question, Dape clears her throat to let him know that he is not dead. She points to a verse in her instructional manual, stating that there is a way to cure what is referred to as HIV, but it's an unconventional remedy. As much as he loves Dape's calm, warming glow, he must confess that things have been shifty with her ever since the very beginning.

She told him that their meeting was going to eventually lead to him getting a record deal, and then the accident happened. Then she said they'd go in to do a short, sweet ritual to plead to the other side for his friend's life, but somehow things took a twist for the negative and now he's the one who might be crossing over some time soon. With his heart still pumping from the news of his fading health, he can't help but bring this to her attention as he asks her for some type of emotional collateral to assure him that she can lead him to this unknown cure for AIDS. Poking out her bottom lip, she thumps her fingers against the worn pages of the book and admits that she understands his uncertainty about this situation right now, yet assures him that the solution is right around the corner if he would just follow the road.

Michael then tells her that that's another thing; there are no corners or a distinct sense of direction for that matter in this never-ending space. It actually feels more like a house of funny mirrors than anything else. And with her slipping in and out of reality without notice, he's just feeling a little uneasy about things right now. She decided to up and leave as he watched his shocking diagnosis of HIV flash before his very eyes.

Dape twists her loose curls around her fingers, pleading with him for his forgiveness in this matter. She then further explains that there are many things that she cannot control since they are not on the earth plane anymore, and her unannounced entry and exit from a scene fall into this category. Therefore, her issuance of an explanation is limited by the ones above who hold the steel set of keys.

He cups his chin between his thumb and index finger, wondering what the hell waits down the road…no consistency…no explanation of crazy events…no nothing! Yet Dape interrupts his rippling imagination right now, as it spirals into the unknown, letting him know that there is a cure in a distant realm, but its price is sort of costly. Pulling out his pockets, he picks a piece of lint from the lining and reminds her that he's completely cashed out right now. Yet Dape beckons for him to come closer and look at the picture she just drew, asking him if he still remembers how to pray.

To his surprise, she has sketched an exact replica of the chapel he used to attend with his grandma back in the day. It even has the purple bell that hangs from the steeple. Dape looks into his eyes, casting forth the waves of memory through his retina, and the colorful image begins to play, recalling a distant time. It's a scene of him and his grandmother as she gives him 5 cents to put in the collection plate. Once inside, the congregation lifts the shimmering, silver tambourines, while the pastor walks down the red velvet aisle. He then steps inside of the pulpit, and as he brushes the powdered donut crumbs off of his tie, he alludes to the fact that today's sermon will tell the tale of the mark of the beast. He sternly shakes his finger; warning how the devil will conquer all nations through the mark of the beast. His grandmamma takes her handheld fan and gently taps his hand, telling him to pay attention to what the man has to say. So little boy Michael lifts his chin up to give him his undivided attention and takes in the message that the mark will be embedded under the skin to identify all the devil's followers.

Pastor Jenkins cups his hand around a goblet and pours an ounce of water into it after he recites the passage in the bible that explains how this branding will saturate the world on a grand scale. He does this action repeatedly to drive his point home, telling the sea of people in the congregation how water is life and that every life lost will be gathered in Satan's cup to make a mockery of the most-high and drown out God's kingdom. And after a sleeping society is collected, the devil will create a stronghold and infiltrate one person to consume an entire flock. So everybody best be on their guard!

Pastor Jenkins takes a tiny eye drop of red food coloring and drops it into the cup to demonstrate just how the mark will multiply across nations and destroy society as a whole. As an eight-year-old boy, Michael sat there on the front pew, eyes fixed on a man in a navy blue suit, with a ponytail swinging, and sweat is dripping down his face. That man spoke with words of wisdom that didn't quite register at that moment. His grandma had handed him a fan to keep cool that day, and although the rest of the church was parched and thirsty for the Holy Ghost, Michael just sat in distilled amazement, with eyes like Bambi, staring at the preacher man who managed to make more than 100 people cry through a cup-sized demonstration. He had almost forgotten about that day, but today, the message is crystal clear.

The visualization of the church slips out of focus, and then pauses itself, returning to the state of a simple Crayola-crafted sketch with a purple bell on the steeple. Michael is now ready to hear the rest of what Dape has to say. She tears the drawing out of her notebook that has the Lord's Prayer written at the bottom of it, handing it to Michael, asking him, "Well, do you remember that tale of the mark of the beast and how he will conquer all nations?"

"Yeah, I think so…"

"Well AIDS is Satan's stepping stone in order to accumulate a perverted human body, millions strong that will be indestructible and composed of numerous souls. But right now, as spiritual beings, we will have the chance to stop him before he's granted his reign on Earth once more and he completely consumes mankind!"

Michael looks at his flesh and can still see a faded imprint of the sentences that had been written all over his body, spiritually encoding his soul with strands of HIV. But now they're merely a shadow as if someone took a big eraser and smudged the majority of the pain away. Though he's still uncertain about his future, he keeps it in his mind that he must remain skeptical about a proposition to not only save his own life, but do so through a medicine that hasn't even been seen before. *No way*, he thinks. *This just can't be right!* He tells himself that AIDS is something kind of new, and those biblical prophecies about the mark of the beast are ancient material…he just doesn't see how they link up. In his mind, it appears that they're simply incompatible.

Dape notices the frown of doubt indented on his face, so she asks him what's the matter and he explains his thoughts to her. Yet skepticism is a natural human trait;

therefore, she advises him from a spiritual standpoint, telling him that a prophecy holds true from the moment that its karma has been conceived in the spiritual realm.

"Karma?" Michael replies in a dazed voice. And she adds, "Yes Michael! Like anything in this world, people get back what they put out. Now there are some horrible secrets that man has kept wrapped away for countless years. But now the truth is unraveling at a rapid speed, and mankind's debt must be repaid immediately. I know it sounds far-fetched, but we need to locate the source of the karma that sparked HIV and kill it before it has enough potency to continually manifest into a giant source of destruction.

"The devil has chosen to take his time and roam right now, and he's seekin' out mass destruction by strategic means with something we human beings ignited years ago in the spiritual realm. It's kind of like his way of coming into eternal power with a poetic bang. Killing a lust-laced culture that's indifferent to night or day as it gently rests upon its fate."

Michael's ears slightly elevate as her speech accelerates, "But now the dark one is sucking down much more energy at a rapid rate and can slay people before they even know that they've been exposed to the virus."

She empties out a sack full of Legos on the dresser top and begins to clasp them together to demonstrate her point. Dape tells him that the demons have figured out a way to tap into the energy realm of global fear, and the layers of negative human emotions are piling up, which is accumulating into mounds of ammunition for the devil to play with. And as she snaps the last Lego in place on the swaying tower, the creation represents fear, and human fear is the fuel that feeds the dark one's cause. It's almost like a type of currency, and the more people worry about AIDS, then the stronger Satan becomes, and he can dig a foothold into innocent lives. And he uses the very thing they fear most to gain strength. And with the recent reports from the CDC, as well as those from the media to promote AIDS awareness, the devil's wishing well of deteriorating health has made him a rich man, one who is cashing in on the world's gathered fear to watch the nations die.

Michael looks her in the eye and says that he sincerely understands her concerns, but insists that AIDS has not progressed to the point where everyone will get it; it's most common among the frequently promiscuous, or just those who catch a bad break in life.

Dape is quiet for a moment, staring down as she stirs her honey tea. Then she goes on to tell him a story. She cups the side of his face and asks him for his assistance in this matter, explaining to him that he has a genetic advantage that will allow him to travel between realms. His ancestors were spiritually sensitive, and the effects trickled down to him. And in this case, he can use his intuitive nature and spiritual gifts to infiltrate the evil one's master plan.

Her tears turn into waterfalls as she cradles herself in his embrace, and he dabs her foggy eyes dry. She then sighs and as she sips from her cup, she admits, "It's only a tablespoon worth of time before the enemy is able to cause HIV to take off and decimate in an airborne fashion! At this point, the virus is too far along in the physical to be manifested out by prayer and fasting alone. Yet the karma that brought the dreary residue of AIDS can be weeded out if someone can first find it and kill it in its point of conception, the spiritual city of Kullah!"

A teardrop skis down the dip of Dape's face, and then lands on Michael's thigh. She goes to brush it off, and this lukewarm liquid against his skin triggers the memory of when the pastor compared the masses of people to a sea of the world's followers that would be captured by the mark of the beast within the last days. His eyes slowly pan up to fully encompass Dape's painful, penetrating pupils, that almost plead for him to understand that this is not just another public service announcement, but it's a fight for our very existence as human beings, both in the here and the hereafter! If Satan were to gain control of us by murdering man with a tool that our karma brought into existence, then the debt of the fallen is later transferred to him, and we are to be his **eternally**!"

There are no words to be spoken right now. It's a choice: the possible fruit of life or a rotting garden of death that's bitter tart devours the man who takes the first bite and passes it along. The two join hands and Dape doesn't say a word, she just chooses to bask in the possibility that a true man will pick up his plight. This concrete concept crystallizes inside Michael's mind, but he is still uncertain about which choice to make.

He pries, asking her first if his friend, Dale, will be okay if he chooses to proceed with this offer, and she tells him that she has the power to tip the scales in his favor through devout prayer and worship, but it is ultimately up to the higher ones to decide a man's final hour.

"The higher ones are very just, but still very strict and they expect a sacrifice before a bed of gifts can be released."

Michael nods his head in agreement with the idea that labor is invested before the payment is rewarded, but he also suggests that any type of physical contract usually dictates the amount of compensation before the worker heads off into the fields. With her hands wide open, she asks him to trust her that the laws are a bit different outside of what he knows as the physical realm, and in this zone, one parallel universe can impact another, and this leaves the results of a conquest in a pending state, and the output of the final prophecy can be drastically changed.

Michael can't help but think of the Super Mario game, and how this new world was beginning to sound either like a conspiracy theory, or a poorly programmed video game. He then asks the golden question, "Well then why me, Dape? If I've got this stuff in me as well, this so-called demonic harvest, then how am I able to weed it out? And secondly, where is this spiritual city called Kullah? I'd love to just follow you through this maze, but I can barely grasp these new rules, let alone promise a sacrifice. Plus, I don't have the foggiest idea where I am going either…"

Dape pours him a cup of tea and tucks his hair behind his ear, letting him know that it takes a human sacrifice in order to be susceptible to this type of spiritual city, which is composed of different energy levels. And this sacrifice is not a rendering of the body. She gently taps her temple, saying, "It's one of a chaste, human mind that has undergone all the cleansing and requirements in order to bend the universal laws to fulfill a hidden prophecy." She goes on to let him know that she understands his nerves at this time, because not only will he be fighting for a greater cause, yet he also has to keep himself in balance as his own life swings in the balance beams. But he will be given some help to accompany his trek throughout existence, almost like when you have a study buddy in detention hall.

She unveils a map of the universe, showing him how the clocks run on a time spell, and that intergalactic gates align together to open hidden channels, portals that encompass the ribbon of each individual's time strip, including the time of now and the tales of history as well. The speed dial just sits there, suspended in the tasteless, protective layer of time, with the negatives of every photographed moment locked within the centuries.

Michael looks at the floor plan of the universe and sees how the pictures of history defy the effects of gravity in a 3-D manner. They are spatially vast and are peppered along an infinite numbers grid, gravitating toward him, slowly, anxious to give him a sneak preview. And all Michael must do is speak a command in order to press play.

He begins to plead with Dape for a deeper level of understanding. He's just not ready to gulp down a mission of such magnitude, and he tells her that his mind definitely isn't pure and chaste. It's filled with sex, the love of booze and all that impure stuff. And if he recalls things correctly, it was a hot, flirty girl who he got into a romp with backstage. It should be apparent that sex and impure stuff gets him into a pickle such as this one in the first place!

Rolling her eyes, Dape helps him understand that in this dimension, time will stand still for him and allow him to slip through the hallways of time to unravel the secrets that brought human beings to the brink of the bridge of life. In this realm, he is not fully human, but not dead either…this is the place of delayed transgressions, where the higher self waits and continues to learn. He is able to complete space travel at ease, and is not in the form of solid flesh, which would delay his ability to walk through walls if he needed to. In here, his body won't decay and crack under the compressed elements like it would on the third planet from the sun. His solar body was designed to remain intact to allow him to search for the key to Kullah to kill the karma before the curse of HIV fully reaps itself to devour mankind.

While gently caressing the curve of his chin, Dape asks him, "You used to see people on the other side when you were younger, didn't you?" Michael looks at his shadow against the textured white walls and lets her know that those were just bad rumors that somehow made their way around town….nothing major..kid talk..ya know?

Dape digs her fist into her hip and verbally orders the 3rd clip from a past summer, the one when he spent the whole season at church camp. The ripples in the sound of her voice have a strong enough vibe to unlock the vault of the year when all the boys had hung their baseball bats, and each one dangled horizontally against the black, iron rack on the closet.

In the clip, Michael was curled up like a sleepy cat, quiet as a mouse. But his eyes began to blink open as he heard a bit of a ruckus in the corner. He snapped his eyelashes shut, trying to tune out the noise because Big Momma had warned him that folks would start talkin' about him, sayin' that he's not screwed on too tight if he started talkin' to others about things that only he is able to see. So he blinks his eyes again…really good this time, in an attempt to ward off any thoughts of things he sees when the lights go off. *Start thinkin' of good stuff,* he coached himself. He thought about the time when his Ma had taken him to the beach and let him play with the seagulls till the tide got really low. Then he shifted to the time when she had walked him to school and they both saw the rainbow, and he asked her if his daycare was at the end of it. He remembers how she just laughed and tucked her hand in her pocket and pulled out a couple of butterscotch kisses to suffice for the treasure they wouldn't be able to reach that day since it was raining so hard.

He tried to tell her how he could see a man crouched over, standing at his doorway as he was goin' to sleep some nights. The man's clothes were sheer rags, and you could kind of see through the guy. In the context of reality, this was simply a ghost, but his mom told him that stuff like that just wasn't real and he'd grow out of this phase in life. When he asked her again how the guy got into his room at night, she just changed the subject, saying they'd better pop the candies in their mouths since the rainbow is still out…for good luck ya' know! He did as she suggested and they counted together, 1-2-3, and then popped the tasty coin candies in their mouths and made a wish in the midst of the sweet colors of the rainbow.

Thinking about stuff like that would usually soothe the sorrow of not being able to comprehend the terrorizing figures of nightfall, at least until he could see the daylight come through the plastic blinds in his room. But it just wasn't working this time. With his pajamas all sweaty, he tried to plug his ears with his fingers, but the rollercoaster of noise in the cabin continually roared in his direction. To get rid of the night sweats, he popped his eyes open and scurried up to the top bunk to wake up Billy. With his chest congested from seasonal allergies, he was panting like crazy, barely breathing. But little Michael was still able to murmur the warning that something in the closet was causing the bat rack to rattle. Billy rubs his eyes and sees his friend all shook up with his eyebrows slanted in fear.

Being brave, Michael pulls his shirt a little above his head and wipes his face off, but when he pulls it back down for a split second, it's like he sees a monster's face instead of his friend's. Michael shakes his head to get a clearer picture of the situation, and then Billy's face begins to unscramble and comes back into clear focus. The noise suddenly stops, so he sits there and tells Billy that he's gonna get a bottle of apple juice from the fridge, and as he begins to climb down the little ladder between their beds, his sweaty palms slip a bit, but he's able to latch onto the sheet on the top bunk and avoid a harsh fall. Placing one foot against the cool, wooden floor, he starts to feel okay, walking a straight line, guided by the line of beds. Placing one foot in front of the other, he looks down and the distance of 5' feels like a homestretch away. But he makes it anyway! Opening the fridge door, the glow from inside the cooler slightly illuminates the room and gives him a chance to do a quick scan to verify that no ghosts or goblins lurk in the corners. He twists open the bottle of juice and while gulping down a sweet swig, he grabs one for his friend and softly closes the ice chest. And then BAM! All crashes down as the bats roll across the smooth, wooden floor, waking up all his teammates.

The lights go on, and a fellow camper asks, "What's goin' on Mikey?" Caught in shock like a cartoon sketch, Little Michael can't help but give a dumbfounded look with his little Juicy Juice lifted in the air. He assures them all that it wasn't him, and shakes his drink as evidence to prove that he was across the room next to the fridge, nowhere near the bat rack.

"Well then who else was it?" another one asks. The little guys are getting grumpy now. They recall how all morning yesterday, Michael swore that he wasn't the one who had been flushing the toilets late at night, but he's the only one that everybody knows doesn't go to bed like the other boys. As a result, he didn't even have enough energy for batting practice the next day. The coach asked Michael to start sleeping in like the rest of the kids and cut out all the shenanigans, so everyone else can get some shut-eye. Still sleepy and too tired to defend himself, he just hung his head and took a nap in the misty sunset till practice was over.

It was clear that people didn't care for his supposed late-night antics, but he is still the guy who was voted as the team captain. Therefore, he found it easier to brush off the hassle and not admit to people that he can really see dead people when everyone else is asleep.

Yet subconsciously, the denial of true events eventually led him to the thought that he processed internally to combat his noir suspicions, which plagued his mind. *Maybe I am imagining all of this*, he would reason with himself. Yet the left part of his brain begged that there had to have been something more to it. Yet as we all know, an accusation without a physical person to tie it to is comparable to throwing a low ball, which was destined to land in the umpire's dusty mitt in the first place…STRIKE!

Meanwhile, the crowd of mini men rally together in the lodge, suggesting that Michael knock it off and stop keeping them up through the night. He chuckles with nerves nestled deep in his little Adam's apple, and then gives his shoulder a rub, promising to keep the noise as low as he can from now on…ya know…for the group's sake.

Michael watches this all from the dimension right outside of Earth, and as the movie stops rolling, his clouded mind peels away and creeps by his side, hovering over a plane above the atmosphere, almost like a cloudy shadow. Then it faithfully crosses the numeric point on the universe's grid so it can fully attach to its owner once more. The childhood memory soon melts away like a Creamsicle on the last day of July, and all focus shifts back to The Chamber of Knowledge, where Dape still awaits an answer from the question she had asked him before he took a cat nap into his hidden past.

She repeats herself, "Michael, as I had asked you…you used to see and hear things that were considered paranormal when you were a boy, right? If I may ask…what made you turn a blind eye to your hidden senses?"

Her fist fits a little firmer into the groove of her hip, and Michael explains how he didn't want his family or his friends to criticize what he was thinking anymore and how it was just easier to make people laugh instead of explaining what he considered to be paranormal events.

Truthfully, people are happier when they are unaware of an immediate presence that could be standing right next to them at the bathroom sink, or as they clean up after Sunday dinner. And they're for damn sure happier not being in the presence of someone claiming to hear voices and see shadows shiver across the floor.

He remembers telling his guidance counselor of the horrific things he could see that actually took place in another dimension that is somehow intertwined with Earth. But the inhabitants of this zone were guarded by a cream-streaked layer that muffled the angry sound waves that visibly bounced around in the other zone's bubbled dome.

Oh yes, he remembers how one day after the guidance counselor offered him a granola bar, she had also given him a warm smile, removed her eye glasses from her steep nasal ridge, and began to talk to him about this calming drug called Ritalin. Her hair bounced a bit, in conjunction with her light-hearted tone. Michael also remembers how her hands were moving in a smooth sequence as she kindly explained how this was a widely accepted remedy that puts troublesome thoughts to rest.

His eyes glistened and his heart sank that day almost like a ship packed to the brim with sandbags of soggy memories. As he grew up, people labeled him as "different;" therefore, adolescence was a very lonely time in his life, and as he extended his hand toward a newfound pal, even if the friendship just lasted a fraction of 5 minutes, he hoped to hear good things from his counselor, such as there were other people like him. This would have somehow blanketed his pain, even if the explanation was purely medical terminology. It's just the thought that someone else out there had felt a similar splinter in the mind that had bled all the way to the heart valve. This way, he could possibly feel a loose link of a connection to someone or something, and then be able to breathe again knowing that somewhere…someone else had gone through the same thing and managed to make it out.

But the guidance counselor did nothing of the sort. After rendering her verdict, her tight lips told a silent and insensitive tale, mocking his sanity, prescribing him pills to make him feel super hungry and continually sleepy.

He remembers being on his knees, begging his mother not to sign the consent form for him to be medicated during school hours as well, but after a board meeting with three other doctors, the school board twisted her arm, and she autographed what she viewed as a path to stop her boy's ragged nerves. She followed the advice of the medical system and allowed them to drug her son to the point of pure sadness. He couldn't go out for recess because the pills made him so sleepy, and he was forced to sit down in the comfy leather chair under the constant supervision of the guidance counselor.

He gained at least 15 pounds around the time of the school dance, and all he would see throughout his junior high halls were the backs of the pretty girls, while they walked away from him. Their ponytails swung in the wind as they overlooked his pudgy image. Down the hall they went every day with their brand new shoes clicking against the tile floor. And as he stared at them, they gave him a glance and quickly made eye contact with him, but managed to raise their binders just a bit to nose-level as they hid their grins behind their folders, wondering if the chunky kid really thought he had a chance. But their slanted eyes penetrated his soul and told the whole story, wondering, *what does this fat kid want from us? Did his mama forget to pack him an extra pork chop or something?*

As Michael detaches from this painful memory, he looks to Dape and asks her for a Kleenex and she pops one out of the box to wipe away his tears. She then sincerely touches Michael's leg and says, "I know that had to have hurt you, honey. Do you need a moment?" He shakes his head and then tells her that there are many reasons why he has chosen to white-out his gift of intuition…the true past is too painful to even verbalize. Dape then takes her finger and it's almost as if it was dipped in ash as she sketches his direct family lineage on a mirror. Here is a picture of all his brothers before they were all separated early on in childhood. His mother was not fully equipped to properly care for a pack of boys; the mental abuse she endured from her father as a kid left her insides feeling like a rusted cuckoo clock. She rarely packed them a balanced lunch, and left them alone in the house for hours at a time as she went on dead-end dates with an array of men who barely reported their last names. She did the best she could, but in the end, Michael was the only one who was left to be cared for by his mother. The solidifying sound of the judge's gabble minimized her parental rights, and she was given a chance to deem herself fit by properly caring for just one boy at a time. She tried so hard, and Michael told everybody how well things were going with his mother just to remain close to her and not end up in foster care.

Meanwhile, at the top of the image is a still shot of his grandpa. He is smiling. He was an extremely happy man, and Dape explains that the gift to see things that are not of this realm extended from their grandfather's bloodline. The power of extreme sight is very powerful if honed just right. And though it skips the odd-numbered generation, it blesses the ones who fall within the even category, which allows him and his siblings to inexplicably know of certain things that happened whether the events had unrolled in ancient Rome, or were scripted in the pages of time to pop up next Thursday morn. The drawing begins to twinkle with animation, and the fragrance of the family tree is edified with colorful strokes. The wonderful aroma is what is making his grandfather smile as he runs through the fields barefoot, soaking up even more of what Mother Earth has to offer. The thought of viewing a clip of a healthy family member lets loose a joyous stream of emotion that Michael has been storing away for so many years.

Dape smiles as she can feel a light begin to blossom within Michael's chest. In between a bitter-sweet reality, something as simple as the image of a happy blood relative sparked a genuine emotion in his solar plexus once more. Dape begins to color between the lines and goes on to explain that if he were to take on this opportunity to conquer AIDS and save millions of lives, especially his own, then he would be accompanied to a sacred city beyond the records of time through a process called past life regression. The special realm is called Kullah, and it is well-hidden as it is intertwined with other galaxy gateways that shuffle the solar frequency without notice. In this case, his keen sense of heightened intuition would be a part of the key that would help him detect the ancient city's location. His genetic legacy is what will fuel his ability to pass though the chapters of his past lives and enter the sacred place.

"Past-life-a-whata?" asks Michael.

Dape takes in a deep breath, sips a bit of her fresh glass of wine, and then picks up again, saying, "Okay, here we go. You're Michael, and you're always gonna be Michael, right here, right now, on every level. But as human beings, we are allowed to undergo many tests, represented by lives lived out on Earth. And with each new test, we get closer and closer to solving our own individual mysteries."

Michael puts his hand to his chin and cannot quite digest the verbiage that he's being fed right now. Not only does he have an incurable case of creeping death within his veins, but he now knows that Dape is saying that most people have lived on Earth more than one time...okay...that's pretty far-fetched!

As Dape's speech speeds up, she explains how past life regression is the only way to satisfy the goal and purify his mind. There is simply no other way to do it! She compares our earthly journeys to a simple test and goes on to underline the fact that most people have failed a couple of times before...it's normal. The concept of life is kinda like the bar exam; no one gets it on the first try—sometimes, not even the second! But the secret that put a dent in society as a whole and caused AIDS lies in one of his past lives. And all he has to do now is retrieve it by mining through the valleys of time to crack the code on the karma that has been maturing for ages. In this case, Michael would be the spiritual alchemist to twist and bend time and help cure the spiritual famine of mankind. Dape then decides to sweeten the deal for him and lets him know that he would not only be saving his own soul, but he could also reverse the curse laid upon his mother by the enemy. She also had fallen victim to this venomous virus. If his mission is completed successfully, then his mother's soul could be released from purgatory and given a pardon.

She points out to Michael that HIV is a generational curse that was given a foothold in his family lineage centuries ago and it continues to haunt his relatives until this day. But through the windows of time, he will be allowed to expediently extinguish this massive murderer...that is if he chooses to pick up this plight. Michael calmly calculates the treasure that shall await him at the end of this journey: a pure life and a freed family. Now if he makes the decision to go in after the prize, then Dale's life could be spared and his mother's life repaired. Plus the song of death would be swept from his lungs as well. Though this may seem like an easy decision, it must be weighed in-depth because in the spirit realm, once you go in, there's no turning back. And who knows what entities might lurk on the other side. In laymen terms, AIDS could be a damn cough compared to the horror that is able to manifest itself beyond the windows of reality.

Dape then removes a suede cloth from an ancient snow globe in her hand. It's engraved with tiny Chinese lettering at its golden stump. Within the protective layer of the dome, a hologram of Michael's mom plays out like a movie bite, and her eyes squint out of distress, while the smoke fogs up the crystal sphere. Michael pivots the piece to face his way, causing a visual eclipse within the snow globe, blocking him from getting a full glimpse of the severity of his mother's situation. Her sweaty palms wipe her forehead, but the beads of perspiration just continue to blister through her scalp and trickle down to her eyebrows.

"She's in the 9th layer," Dape explains. Now the 9th layer is the cottony part that lines the layer right above the cocaine-colored flames, also referred to as the threshold of hell. It is pure steam down there…not even something one could measure by Celsius degrees.

"What can I do Dape?" Michael asks, stroking the smooth surface of the globe's cool exterior. But the perspiration from his fingertips soon evaporates as the glass reaches Fahrenheit 451, sending up vapors of steam from common contact. And as a natural reaction, Michael instantly retracts his right hand. Meanwhile, pulling out a handheld first aid kit, Dape reaches for his palm and pulls it close to her midsection, slowly swabbing only those fingers that are painfully red. She sorrowfully informs him that even after his mother's crossing, she still didn't get free the way she needs to be! She, as well as the others, dwindles in the web of debt, which has been woven by the dark one. The enemy has been slowly draining her veins, feasting off her diminishing vigor, causing her to weep in pain and wheeze as she wilts, searching within her belly for enough strength to hang on…just for one more day. She and many others in the dangerous afterlife panic on a daily basis, as they are disabled by the pending contract of HIV. The devil clutches her heart with a sinister form of repayment as her mind is constantly subjected to the hands of his demonic debt collectors. They are forever permitted to torture those who have fallen victim to the three-letter curse, draining their energy levels and slowly feasting on a number of people, starting from the skin of their feet and eventually hoping to progress to the tender flesh of one's eye sockets. This is permitted throughout the coal-colored gates that guard the devil's kingdom…that is unless the karma that ignited the destruction of human DNA is crushed, breaking Satan's binding curse.

Michael doubtingly looks at Dape, saying, "But in order to cure this thing, you want me to repeat lives that I've already failed in before? I don't know about life for you, Dape, but to me it's been pretty miserable. I lost my mother right when our family was about to get back on track. My life has since been derailed, and some days I can barely scrape together enough pocket change to pay my house note…let alone all the utilities. And the only guy I've ever been able to trust in my life is in a hospital bed, barely making waves on the heart monitor.

"Plus if I didn't get this thing called life right in the past, then what makes you think I'm gonna pass the exam now? If life is just like a test, then I got a 21 the first time I took the ACT back in my high school days, and then I got an 18 when I took it again. If there's a lot riding on this gamble, then maybe we can do something pretty mellow…kinda like a pre-test, and then I can take the real test. Meanwhile, we'll only record the better score, ya know?" Dape gives him a smirk yet still says nothing. Frustrated, he scratches his head and then continues, "So has Jesus ever been known to give out a little cheat sheet for his faithful students?"

Her smile curls a little bit more. She is tickled that he still possesses a little sense of humor in the midst of this massive decision. Then, as if he didn't already know, she reminds him that he would not only be saving his mother's soul, but his own life as well!

And although life isn't all that great right now, the intermittent, drearier side of his brain begins to ponder how bad it would be to go to the other side right now. Yet the suffering image of his mother moaning on the beach of hell brings him back to his senses, and he knows what he needs to do. He combs Dape's bank of knowledge for encouragement in this process, asking her if it's a common thing for an individual to have had more than one lifetime. She nods her head and explains that pretty much 98 percent of the human population has had a past life before, even if their lives were extremely brief, such as in the case of a stillborn. She goes on to tell him that God is not the man behind the iron curtain. He's strong. He's firm, but he understands that life is an obstacle course and it's easy for people to get tangled up in the net. She brings him back to the concept of family, and lets him know that the Lord holds a special place for him in his heart because he basically had to raise himself. Therefore, he is a stronger person for it. He had the will to still make something happen for himself in this world, and God's gonna see him through the rest of the way. See, the average person is tied to a lineage, and the siblings bind together and help each other out to make things easier for the future generations.

But even with family; even with money; even with love; it's easy for the dark one to take on many forms and deceive the innocent, and that's why a lot of times you get to pass go twice in the game of life.

Michael slants down along the barely visible yet sturdy walls in this room and thinks about how daunting of a task this could be. Not a lot of people make it out of the course of life, and he recalls in the scriptures how it says that the mouth of hell has been known to widen itself just to gulp down another batch of souls. He tries to find a way to escape going back through those lives that he's already been known to have failed in, and he asks Dape about the supposed 2 percent of people who didn't have to repeat life on Earth. They are in heaven, and he wonders what they did right so he can pick up some tips. Then he ponders this concept. He tells her that they obviously got it right and probably have some type of answer key, so why can't she let them spin the wheel in this game of life?

Dape replies to his attempt to wiggle free from an unknown fortune, explaining how those people are in sacred consecration with the holy ones as we speak. So once in heaven, their mortal lives are finished, and in order to reach the center of the hidden city of Kullah, it takes a *human* sacrifice of the *mind* to unlock the chamber!

No matter how sad he thinks the symphony of his life has played out, being a human being, who is still suspended in the Now Time of reality, grants him certain privileges. As a mortal man, his distinct composition of mind, body and soul is allowed to fall into perfect sequence and precisely align with the other timing dimensions that are still in progress. The trinity of a man was designed perfectly for time travel!

He begins to jam his hand in his pocket, scratching the back of his neck as he bites his bottom lip, trying to whip up enough courage to clarify to her that he just might not be the man for this job. He blurts out, "Life is pain, Dape! We both kind of know that! Do you really think I wanna fumble outta bed again knowing what has already happened in the past? That's torture to know that in a couple of seconds I'm destined to stub my toe again, or better yet, to see myself running through a script where I know that it's in my little time schedule that I'll roam through the back alleys looking to sell a glad bag of 12-dollar weed to make ends meet. The future is inescapable, and no matter what I do, I'm gonna end up short on my house note and there ain't a damn thing I can do to stop it?" He touches the side of her face, only to explain that he just can't imagine putting himself through that kind of stuff again. Reliving that crap would feel like holding a universal remote control, but the play button is jammed, and there's no way to skip those annoying commercials…ya know?

Dape then grabs the Life manual and points to all the possibilities to succeed, assuring him that if he goes back into his past lives, not his present one, then he could prevail. But how he deals with the decisions he's about to make a second time around will determine the future of society, and he could live again without the residue of HIV. Plus, as he attaches himself to the consciousness of another time zone, he will be unable to know of the upcoming events that have already played out in his past lives. He is going to be engulfed in the centuries of the past, and it'll be like his memory is a blank slate that is ready to conquer a new day! As Michael's head droops like a leaky hose, he weighs the decisions he's made up to this point and ponders the thought: Sure…if he locates the karma that stirred up the AIDS virus, then he would be allowed to live, but what's he got left to live for? His mom died years ago. His brothers are all in jail, and only one is scheduled for a hearing to determine if it's okay that he leaves the joint to go to a mental ward!

He rationalizes the decision to forfeit the opportunity to spare his own life and the lives of others. He thinks that if he goes to confession on a regular basis, then he could just let nature take its course as his body gives out. But at least he'd be given a green light to get into heaven this way. Sure, it wouldn't be that great defecating a fistful of pills day in and day out, but at least the pain would eventually subside upon expiration. Not knowing what lies ahead in his past lives is a terrifying thought!

Then Michael remembers the bargaining price that's attached to his blood flow right now. If all of his newfound knowledge is really true, then he owes Satan for biting of the blackened fruit. And the place where that guy lives is hot. Kids used to joke around in the neighborhood that the devil digs his claws into the cement walls of hell, ripping out the A/C in the main lobby. Plus, it's rumored that his waiting room is constantly in flames.

As Dape closes the compilation of his life scripts, she makes a second plea, insisting, "If for no one else, do it for your mother, Michael! You know you loved her, and I know it must've hurt like hell to have lost her at such a young age. But if you do this thing right, then you both will be able to see each other again, and the curse of the blackened chain will crumble."

Michael looks down at his feet, and he fills the white space between his shoes with the visualization of his mother and how they used to play for hours when he was a kid. He recalls the times when she was excited about life and would sometimes spread the peanut butter and jelly across the soft, buttered slices of bread. Oh how it would taste so good, and Ma used to seal it up really tight with those double-lock bags just to make sure it carried the same freshness all day long until the school bell rang and it was time to go to lunch with the other kiddos. These good memories made up for the other ones.

The tear drops from his eyes fall onto his unlaced loafers, making water dots on their blue jean fabric. This is a lot to swallow right now, so he pops in a cube of chewing gum and paces clear down the hall. In the elongated portal, the energy level shifts to a different frequency as he gains speed and eases down the numeric grid. His mind melts with his old memories and somehow his mental frequency is projected onto the blank canvass of the wall. Framed still shots of his mother and brothers are allowed to play in motion for about 10 seconds at a time. He remembers the time when his brother, Dougie, taught him how to double-tie his shoes. Then a ghostly clip plays, showing how they all climbed the neighbor's brick steps in costume the night when they went trick-or-treating together. Somewhere between munching on Kit Kats and knocking on random neighborhood doors, they all stayed connected in the still black of the night by using hand-held walkie-talkies.

The reruns of his life memories are all framed with shimmering silver, and a rare smile sneaks across the lower half of his face as he recalls the slim window in time when he was still happy. His heart begins to bulge with childhood euphoria like an overstuffed family photo album. All his siblings are dispersed across creation right now, and the only "family" he seems to have left is his friend Dale who always told him that his couch was open if he ever needed a place to stay.

As he passes through the negative hall of numbers within the portal, he leaves the pictures of his past behind him, entering a dim, damp, sectioned-off hallway. And as he moves along the number scale, the movement is comparable to the motion he felt years ago when he boarded his first plane at the airport. To the human eye, the door at the end is locked shut as a neon light outlines its rectangular shape. It appears to be almost a quarter of a mile away, and its size hints that it could fit onto the hinges of a small girl's playhouse. But once Michael leans forward and pokes his nose beyond the mist, his face emerges through the fog as he realizes that the next portal is only an arm's length away. The fog distorted his perception, but now he can see that the door is roughly 8 x 2.5 x 8 feet. As he reaches for the doorknob, a bass-ridden voice chuckles, and the vibration waves echo like a game of ping pong between Michael's ears. Then the crimson chalk lettering writes a ghostly, vertically-positioned message right below the foggy window of the doorway, asking: ***WHO ARE YOU?***

Michael looks over his shoulder, only to realize that Dape is no longer present, and as he attempts to answer this question, he can't help but notice that his own voice is collapsing into a mute box in light of the compressed energy field that he just transitioned into during his shift to another frequency level. The air is almost at zero here, and he does not have enough oxygen in his lungs to muster a reply right now. All he can do is simply breathe slowly through his nose while he turns sideways to make sure he can fit through the narrow doorway.

The writing on the portal then shakes about like an Etch-A-Sketch, and a new question appears: ***Do You Want To See Your Mother Again?*** The lettering is copied in blue this time as the grinding sound of an unlocking key hole sends waves throughout the hallway. But all noise bounces back against the door once it reaches the central point of Zero, the numeric location that Michael had recently passed up. The crescendo of sound continues to ricochet throughout the white veils hanging in the zone right now. Then the ominous door creeks as it opens, letting loose a neon glow composed of electricity. Its intensity would engulf anyone close enough to witness even the slightest glimmer of its radiance as it sends Michael's hair flying back. He turns his head and closes his eyes, and then like magic, pale bricks…pitch white as snow…pop up through the floor to place his feet on solid ground, as if he were standing upon new cement, forming a new pathway, which disappears as it is swallowed by the source of the light beyond the thick, wooden door.

Michael sighs and thinks about the offer he's been given to deliver his generation from the ultimate plague, as well as the chance to save his own soul.

From a distance, Dape sees that he is struggling a bit with this extremely foreign environment, so she emerges from a hidden corner and runs through the smoky hall to hold his hand and make sure his feet are planted as firmly as can be while travelling through this dimensional tunnel. Not knowing where else to turn in the midst of this uncertainty, he kisses her damp hand and makes a firm plea for compensation once his plight is completed. He wipes his forehead while reiterating that he desires for his mama to be cured of this plague…with her soul fully replenished and rescued. But as the wind rapidly rips by his jittery jaw line, he pants between his sentences, insisting, "If I make it through, then I want Dale to make it through his surgery, too, as well as a record label when this curse…I mean this virus…is over!"

Dape smiles, while nodding profusely, and the second that he completes this contract, a see-through red carpet unrolls in a crisscross fashion over the pavement. So he plants his foot firmly against its grainy material, ducking down, while bracing himself for a second helping of the oncoming winds. And as the light pales, his celestial body reaches a higher frequency, whiting out the visibility of anything else in sight.

CHAPTER Three

The First Portal

Before the transportation, Michael and Dape were basking in the elements of what is called the ether. This is the thin, stretchy material, laced with electric currents, that lies just a tad beyond Earth's atmosphere, bending right before the point of the outer limits. The frequency of this layer is compressed next to Earth, right before the horizons of outer space stretch toward the heavens. Here is where the tiny, baby blue beads of energy surge throughout its streaming lines of electricity, mimicking the imagery of a coded video game. The ether is the place where all ideas and inventions pass before they are manifested into a physical reality upon the earth plane. All things also exit the earth plane in a similar fashion.

And at this current moment in the spiritual realm, Dape and Michael still possess the imperative layers of themselves to travel. Their current bodies are a combination of mind and soul right now at a sort of jellied state. The pair is in what is referred to as the white-out phase, where one's shell is not fully solidified such as a 3-D manifestation would be if it were physically residing on the earth plane. See, the layers of self fade away, slowly, as one peels away from Earth and moves into the outer dimensions, while phasing through the ether, and so forth. The body is meant to carry the soul for a short duration on Earth, and then the mind maintains the transitional balance, while self endures the transition as it is simultaneously engulfed by heaven's bosom.

Think of it as if the animators of this scene had flipped their pencils and gently brushed an eraser across Dape and Mike a few times. This is what happens when one exits Earth and no longer needs a fully solidified body. The visual manifestation of self thins out, while pieces of one's trinity attach to a new form of existence. Michael and Dape still possess the mental capability to project forth a celestial form of themselves throughout their temporary stay in the ether zone. Yet the threads of self have worn thin in the ether as well. They pretty much have in a way visualized themselves into a new type of existence, while subtracting the element of the 3-D body from the triple-self composition. But now the two sit in the Chamber of Knowledge Part II, which lies on the purest radius in the spiritual realm. Dape smiles at Michael as she taps her giant medicine cabinet, which is fully set up for operation. Right now, the visual manifestation of their bodies is see-through, and Michael's eyes play ping pong as he tries to get his thought waves to sync with this new, jellied form of existence. Dape has some color to her, but she is still translucent. Her honey skin bears the tone that comes about as if someone had simply released two drops of coloring into a firming jelly mixture and gifted her with a similar complexion.

In the spirit realm, her skin and clothing are as see-through as linen that's been worn thin, swaying in the sunlight. Her frequency has now reached a fully spiritual composition as her hourglass figure flutters around to unlock a pyramid-shaped medicine cabinet that's about 10-feet tall. While cradling the lock with a napkin in her hand, she spins the sacred combination in a numeric sequence until it loosens and falls to give her full access. Across the way, Michael's soul is nestled deeply in a red velvet movie chair with a bag of popcorn in his left and the soda in his right. Dape looks over her shoulder and smiles at him, asking, "So what do you think of the place so far?"

He replies, "I think you did a bang-up job, here," while lifting the goblet her way for a toast. Black velvet curtains drape the private theatre and frames of his family members decorate the walls as they are lined in silver artistry.

She lets him know that the universal remote is in his seat pocket to the right, but the screening is also voice-enabled for his viewing pleasure. He can just say things like "Stop," "Go Back," or "Summary" if things go too fast. Dape puts the lock on the countertop and pulls back the 10-foot long doors of the pyramid-shaped medicine cabinet to reveal a galaxy of stars. Now when you first look at the triangle of vast space, speckled with tiny stars, it brings back the memory of a clear, summery night, while staring up at the stars, guessing which one is Venus, Orion's Belt and so forth. Yet with the flicker of the switch at the end of the wall, Dape is able to dim the lights and demonstrate how some universes interact with one another, while still maintaining separate frequency levels. As she turns the switch off and on again, the connect-the-dot imagery is edified by loud purple lines, mapping out a hidden galaxy quest. The dots are also connected by lines of neon light, and the lights switch positioning upon command as multiple universes are outlined in green. It is revealed how some paired universes operate off of each other's gravitational pull, and the extreme difference in the energy frequencies does not demagnetize these zones thanks to an unidentified regulator called dark matter, which feels like putty if one were to reach out and touch it. This "glue" feels almost like the kind that can be found on the back of an architect's stack of post-its. Within this zone, as multiple layers are peeled away, there continually lies another frequency level, which is governed by another parallel universe's rule book.

Dape shows him the hidden entryways, certain laws tied to space travel and the overall grid of outer space. She then walks closer to the pyramid, with a mini crowbar in-hand, and stations her right leg on the edge of the shape to get a firm grip. And with her left foot firmly planted on the carpeting, she manages to reshape the pyramid into a rectangle, dinging out any form of curvature, until the form of an aquarium can be clearly identified. Popping her knuckles, Dape further instructs Michael that all of outer space is enclosed within a type of aquarium, and this rectangular zone houses all the mini worlds.

Within the outer limits, the soul can travel freely, but the gamer must first learn the playbook. As he watches a series of instructional clips, Michael's eyelids flutter almost 20 times in half a minute. He intermittently feels feint, absorbing layers worth of knowledge at a time. Dape schools him in 20 different topics, letting him know that he will not need to travel to these distant worlds, but it is important to know how they all rely on one another to automatically play off of the other's frequency levels. This way, his spirit will have an advantage to navigate the earth plane in record timing.

Then he learns about the time reel and how everyone and everything holds an indentation in the past, present and future. When he comes back into the earth zone, he will have access to a number of time reels, especially those tied to his past lives. Once the mind has been purified to a specified point, he can then gain access to the holy city of Kullah, where the karma that created HIV still festers.

Michael asks her what he needs to do once he is inside the sacred space, and she smiles at him, letting him know that many pieces of the puzzle will only align and make sense once he is in conjunction with the correct frequency of time.

This is all mesmerizing as he processes the concept of time. Drumming his fingers on his pant leg, he finds an optimistic melody that reminds him to keep a beat with the wrinkling ripple of time. Things seem surreal here, and the concepts initially register as vague but later develop in clarity. Who ever knew that all these jagged pieces would fit together into a puzzle called reality…the secret world of reality!

But this is not all fun and games. There will be a need for sacrifice in order to collect due payment and fulfill the prophecy. Dape then grabs a small bottle of medicine from the rectangle's side cabinet and says, "Now are you ready to see the secrets of the past?"

Michael nods his head in great anticipation, begging to hear more about this fantasy that seems to be tied in with a tucked-away sliver of reality.

As she walks up to him, she bends down to look him in the eye and puts her hand on top of his, saying, "Now you know I have your best interest at heart, right?" He lets her know that he trusts her right now as she radiates an angelic hue. She places her fingertip on top of the open bottle of elixir until a little dab of its red oil runs onto her skin. She explains how he might feel a slight sting as she rubs the purification remedy across his closed eyelids. He smiles and bounces a little bit in his seat, wondering what could be more painful than the time when he got his first tattoo. He was 17, and he took a few swigs of Jack Daniels to drown out the pain until it was all over. He almost teases her, waving his hand while giving her a mischievous wink. "Go ahead!" he says… "I dare you!" And with his boyish grin, she proceeds to wipe traces of the healing liquid on top of his twitching eyelids. Yet the pain is stronger than what he had imagined. The potency of the stinging mint causes his eyes to water as if someone had cut a huge, white onion right beneath his nose. His mental imagery spirals into a pitch white funnel cloud, and the carpet ride to the past begins to take off!

His jellied soul serves as a cup holder of his spirit. They are in a sense separate, but they operate in unison as well. Now as the soul remains seated in the chair, the spirit takes off like a comet, launching toward the rectangle. A movie screen then drops down, filling the emptiness of the shape, and his spirit slowly penetrates the veil's putty-like consistency. And as Michael burrows through the chill of the screen, frozen chips fly off of it upon penetration.

Two minutes later, his spirit is in there, squiggling around like a fresh tadpole that is suspended in existence. Then the immediate growth spurt takes place. What usually happens in the years of a boy's puberty lets loose in about 60 seconds, yet he is growing in a spiritual sense this time. Michael is undergoing a spiritual rebirth as he hatches into his stronger self. As crisp water rains down on him from above, Michael simply slicks his hair back behind his ears as mind, body and soul further compress in this dimension and increase in strength.

The lights go dim, but then things brighten up again as he looks around a room with four distinct walls. A globe sits on the desk, and a bookcase is directly behind him. But it is all transparent because in the land of the universe, the different planes of mind vs. reality can easily collide within the galaxies that mesh with the layers of the mind. They often overlap one another, and it sometimes becomes difficult to differentiate the rugged texture of reality. Yet one thing is apparent. As Michael's eyes shift a bit to the right, he is able to see through the transparent wall separating him from his soul-self, which is still in the chair in front of the big screen. There his sleeping self sits in that movie theatre, with his head gently resting against his palm. It almost appears as if he fell asleep while watching a long movie. The truth is that upon entry into the battlefield of the mind, he was put into a temporary state of rest. See all selves are linked: Mind. Body. And Spirit/Soul. They all were intended to operate within a harmonic fashion, but when one goes through a traumatic event or falls into a state of depression; the spirit usually has to wait until all three clocks of self are synchronized again to continue in motion.

This immediate transition was a lot for him to take in, but from the inside of the screen, Michael balls his hand into a fist and scrubs against the veil in a circular motion with the intention to wipe the fog off and continue viewing the image of his soul that is still paused in the spiritual realm. But this thin type of film is not wiping clean. It's caked up against the gloss and won't go anywhere. Then a subtle vibration begins to rupture beneath Michael's feet, and he takes one foot and stacks it on top of the right one as he looks from side to side in a sea of sudden darkness. He blinks twice, even three times in hope of seeing someone else in sight. But all that is illuminated is the soulful image of his still shot on the other side. Meanwhile, the sides of the dimension that are enclosed within the giant entertainment center begin to streak like running paint. It feels like it's raining, yet the steady drops seem to have evaporated.

Slowly, the scene walls begin to melt, and the floor buckles. Michael crouches down, both hands on the ground, and stares upward toward the opium-tinted light. Then like a spinning top, the room rotates counterclockwise, and it scares the living daylights out of Mike. He doesn't know what's going on, or if this is a scheduled ghost ride or what! His voice echoes as he asks Dape if she could possibly slow this thing down for a moment, but the friction only picks up until the trap door flies open from the bottom. As he falls one-thousand feet, the gust of horizontal wind slows his oncoming speed, allowing his bare body to come down as a gentle kite. And as he skydives through the layers of existence, it dawns on him that if he pulls his legs together in a linear fashion, while cupping his hands, this would give him more navigational pull. All fear has left his body as his cheeks ripple in the wind.

Maintaining a sturdy posture, he just pushes forward and as he nears a section in this dimension that appears to be brightening up, he sees rays of light again, glistening over sparkling tan sand. He tilts himself to a side angle and curls up into ball form, falling at a bit more of a faster rate. Then it occurs to Michael that this could all just be a mental journey, so what is there to fear? Yet one can still get injured from mental trauma…right? He takes a chance and decides to do things that he wouldn't normally do while enwrapped in a 3-D reality. Stretching his body out again, he comes crashing down onto the time ripple of ancient Mexico, and he lifts his head in amazement since he can still move his body around as if the sudden impact never even happened. Though he spits out a mouthful of sand, he has a smooth conscience…knowing that he tried what was once the unthinkable. He stands up and greets an oval, string portal, which is one-dimensional in depth. It is elevated off the ground and has a magnetic frequency, which draws him closer to its presence like a moth to a 1000 Watt flashlight. The light cascades off the portal's metallic silver surface, and his eyes just keep going up to take in its full beauty.

Moving a bit to the left, he leans forward enough to witness that it's a circular shape that is as flat as a piece of paper. It hovers just a couple of feet above ground in the middle of a desert. As he walks closer to this terrestrial wonder, curiosity bids him to just touch its silver waves. But before he does this, he hears a sly voice whisper, "Hi there, Michael. How are things going?"

Oh damn is the only thing running through Michael's thought waves right now. The vibration of those vocal cords sounded like the commentary from an Alfred Hitchcock flick. And anyone with that kind of voice had to have smoked like a thousand cigarettes down to the filter to mumble that type of greeting.

Before he turns around, Michael makes sure he has a smile reflecting all his teeth before facing whatever lurks in the distance.

He turns around, but can't really see anything. Yet what appears to be a mirage slowly formulates before his bright eyes. The sand whisks together and twists into a mini storm.

Then, as it all packs together, a pair of eyes are etched into this freshly crafted sculpture, and a jaw line is then created as the rest of a jaguar's features are filled in.

A thin wisp of air then glides by Michael's stomach and rushes over the sculpture, chiseling the animal's teeth into place, and the figure then cracks a smile with its left eyebrow heightened, asking "So what do you want?"

With the mind's eye, Mike can now see how the manifestation of existence lies on a numeric grid. Translucent numbers stream vertically on a projection of a grid behind the animal. Though he sees a lot of zeros and possible solutions to an equation, he hasn't gotta clue what he needs to say right now. The figurine comes into full focus. Michael tucks his chin deep into his neck as the jaguar giggles a bit, asking him what he's thinking right now.

Michael scans the atmosphere a bit more and asks him why this all looks like a programming script for a video game or something, and the creature laughs. Michael is able to roll his shoulders back as he feels the sludge of the mood disintegrating.

"Well, these are all your thoughts," the animal-man suggests. The being adds, "But they're coded and have been kept for centuries at a time ya know?" Michael lets him know that he's flattered by the idea that his laundry list of loose ideas are worthy of such publication, but he beckons the jaguar to tell him where the real deal is…the hidden city of Kullah. The being then slants his eyes, shocked by his subject's pure boldness. Yet he points at the one-dimensional gateway, explaining that this is the entry point and merely the first step. The being then goes on to ask forgiveness for forgetting his manners as he introduces himself as Surai. Suddenly, as the being smiles and winks, a glass appears in Michael's hand, but it is empty. He asks him where the rest of the water is, and Surai lets him know that this is merely intended to be a measuring tool in this virtual reality, and its image will always display in his mind's eye. The closer he gets to Kullah, then the faster the water will rise to the brim, and when he finds the cure for the virus…he shall never have to suffer from thirst again.

Michael compliments his metaphoric manner of speaking, but drops the glass on the sand, not wanting to take a gift from such a murky looking creature. But he makes up an excuse and says that he usually prefers to drink from his cupped hands…it just feels more natural. But he does ask him where he can find an actual swig of H2O in the meantime. He puts his hand in his pocket, and although this is the most awkward situation, holding a full-fledge conversation with an animal that talks, he doesn't dare lose composure in the face of fear. So Michael perks up his ears and continues to listen as the beast lets him know that on the mental forefront, there is water that never runs dry. Whatever he chooses to manifest shall be. So Michael closes his eyes and gets a clear image of a waterfall, but as he opens his eyes again, there doesn't appear to be anything in the water glass.

Then Surai asks him to remember the time when he ran track in high school and all he could see was that giant water cooler at practice. He asks him to generate those same feelings again. Michael's tongue feels like a sponge, so he desperately closes his eyes and visualizes his Nike cleats tearing up the freshly trimmed grass back in the day. And even though the sun was whiting out his vision, he just kept going up that grassy knoll until he wound up at the orange and white water cooler. He kneeled down and didn't even use a cup while stationing himself under the spout, letting the cool stream run over his chapped lips.

That's it…that's it! He starts to feel the memory that comes from the quench of ages rush down his chin, and it runs over his shoulders as it continues to trickle down. But as he opens his eyes, his cupped hands only have about an ounce and a half of H2O in them. Meanwhile, his energy levels have reached a high enough spiritual peak to penetrate the spiritual realm of manifestation, but he wonders when the rest of the water is gonna come into this realm of existence! He feels some type of hydration tingle within his cells, but this is all a part of the emotional cultivation that comes when channeling a product into the atmosphere. He feels the effects of the visualization process, yet hasn't even taken a sip. And still he wants more. What he managed to manifest so far wouldn't even satisfy a baby. Surai can't help but address the confusion written on Michael's face right now.

He explains, "See Michael, mind, body, and then soul work as one, but you are currently in three different divisions right now. You mentally satisfied your drought in the dimension of your mind, but even if you were to take a swig of what you have before you, you wouldn't be able to wholly devour it. Your selves are separated right now, but if you travel through the portal, then you can temporarily marry your mind with yourself again to navigate through time and touch base with elements of your body in the earth realm. You are not in physical form right now, so you do not need H2O to survive. Yet your thirst for satisfaction will be truly quenched after you endure the process of past life regression."

He rolls his eyes and explains to Surai how he just went through some disgusting jelly substance, and the shock of all these instances is still very real in his mind. Therefore, this type of emotional exertion should serve as the equivalent for at least one past life regression.

Surai chuckles heavily and then opens his mouth as Michael's sight veers down the being's tonsils to witness a sea of miniature people swimming in his saliva, moaning aloud. The scorching state of their bodies only raises the temperature of their blistering bath water, sending steam through Surai's nostrils. He snaps his mouth shut and Michael's chin drops in amazement. Could it be that this jaguar is representative of the dark one? As Surai closes his mouth, Michael asks who those people were. Surai casually clears his throat and briefly explains that those folks had a tab that had to be paid…nothing personal. The jaguar smiles, but the vibe he exuberates is sinister and unsettling, bringing about the same effect that comes from sipping sewage water. But he dares Michael to try and outrun the plague and shoot for his godly goal. He confesses that he is fond of watching many men try and outwit a game in which he already knows the majority of the secret codes and rules for.

Michael cringes at the thought of who he may be engaged in loose association with right now. Clearing his parched throat, his voice cracks and his vocal cords wobble a bit, while he calmly asks Surai to reveal his true identity.

The being replies, "I used to have a nice bed in heaven and sing at the dawn of every new day with the other angels. Then they threw me out and now I just travel from place to place, kinda like this, finding entry points along the frontlines of the mind." He kindly smiles and redirects Michael to the portal that will lead him closer to see if he can claim the rite of passage to Kullah. He gulps a bit and slowly shuffles toward the shadow of the portal.

He sticks his hand inside this one-dimensional portal and can feel currents buzzing about, causing his fingernails to bend inward and curl. Then the electricity that radiates from the gateway stirs heat waves from his wrist to the forearm. His eyes dilate as his brainwaves race to catch up with this unknown electric static. The messages that are usually sent from the synapses, which are located in the brain, seem to be delayed. And although the current has already made its way up Michael's forearm, the majority of the energy seems to be pressing against the elbow, a part of his arm that is not enclosed in the star gate. In this energy field, the mind conjoins with the spirit again to temporarily grant access to the transmitter between the planes of reality. These places are all governed by time and distance.

Night creeps into the picture, and as the moon rises from behind the trees, its glow glistens across the ripples of Mike's muscular back, while he witnesses Surai decay like a dry sand castle. The sandy particles, which once crafted the jaguar, fall and reunite with the grainy ground, and Michael becomes aware of a sly presence hovering behind him. All of a sudden, he can allow communication to flow from his brain and flood the rest of his body with prompts to remove his forearm from the dimension and spin around to see what the matter is.

While he turns around, the wind blows against his face, causing the slimy residue from the slippery portal to drip onto the sand for fast absorption. Above him comes more mental imagery meshed into full focus, and in the center of the moon, a crowd of people start to heckle at the sight of a dazed Michael who has been brought to the point of watery eyes. In their clan, it has been rumored that Mike is the man responsible for more than one-thousand deaths in their tribe!

As the ghostly image floats closer to the ground on a cloud of white smoke, a dingy skeleton lady with white, frayed hair, puts her hands on her hips and taunts, "Hey Jose, you thought you had us beat a long time ago, didn't you? You did all of this to us, but now you're gonna pay for your sins!" She puts her jewel-studded headdress on, and it is radiant with bundles of peacock feathers. The lady smiles and with the shake of her head and the clank of her chunky, silver earrings, she plants her bony feet firmly apart and bounces first up then down, spinning her head around and around to conjure up enough energy to invoke a super spell. Her torso moves in an S-fashion, like a stretchy accordion, making sure to exert enough energy so the spell comes out just right. The rest of the folks laugh as their hands, covered with ruby rings, flutter over the damsel's skeletal curves to support her method of witchy energy channeling. They sing, *Step inside, step inside of our story. Come inside, so we can repay you!*

Michael looks at these bony people who appear to have emerged from the grave, and wiping a sandy moustache from the creases of his mouth, he asks to speak with the lady, one-on-one, to assure her that he holds no debt to her.

Her eyes hone in on him like a serpent in the presence of a rat, and her fangs ferociously unfurl as she feels the spirit of her ancestors surge through her chest. Dusty winds whip through her aura as she extends her arms, winding them in a circular motion to get the mood just right. Moving them about like sequenced windmills, they constantly cross one another and move extremely fast to give off the illusion that she's working with six extra arms.

In the meantime, her silver necklace begins to radiate as her energy reaches boiling point. At first the reflection from the medallion was kind of dim. But as she gains speed, its reflective capabilities stretch closer and closer toward Michael as she births a chant from the pit of her belly, managing to launch it through her vibrating tonsils. The gust of wind knocks Michael onto his back, and as he continues to tumble, he then slams sideways against the oval, one-dimensional portal. He is then compressed by the gravitational pull from the other side of the metallic gateway and takes on a semi-fetal position as he is being sucked into its magnetic wavelength. The Mayan pyramids draw closer to one another, and the square windows radiate in a bingo sequence. One window lights up on the stone-paved first story, and in a sense, it catches fire from level to level until all the windows, including the ones on the very top floor, come aglow. The wattage from the colossal creation shifted from giving off a dim illumination to shimmering with an abundant capacity for light, and its effect mimics the visual glow from extremely toxic radiation exposure. The matte-finished moon spins on the axis of midnight, while the complexion of the one-dimensional portal churns into a deep gray. As Michael is fully forced into the one-dimensional portal, he embarks on a new scene that opens across the warm waters blue.

CHAPTER Four

Ambush

Ancient Mexico. The Yucatan.

Now completely consumed by what is called the third dimensional portal, which serves to untie the ribbon to the past, Michael's spirit has meshed with the mental memory of his past life that he formerly lived as Jose. As a great captain in the ranks of the Spanish fleet, he was faithfully known as that cheery guy with ripe, red cheeks. He's fun…always patting a bud on the shoulder with a good joke or two and is known to grab his fellow sailor a wooden pint-cup to pour him a rush of cultured rose wine. It would splash to the top, bustling over the brim. And while leaning his leg on the tabletop, he would proceed to puff his chest out and brag of his past plunder, which was purchased through succulent slaughter of fallen enemies.

All would laugh as he reminisced upon the times when he outwitted his poor prey. Groups would run across the green, dandelion-studded meadows, trying to remember the direction from whence they had first come. They scratched their heads with scrambled eyes, trying to remember the location of the great oak that had a black slash painted across the tree trunk. This was their landmark that was intended to point the way home. But little did they know that prior to their arrival, Jose had marked at least three or four trees with the same embellished tick mark to throw off his prey's sense of direction.

As he stalked the helpless, he found it funny how they'd let out a sigh of relief after finding that familiarly marked tree. It was one of the first things that they had seen upon entering the dark forest, so human logic led them to believe that their villages couldn't be too far away.

Yet worry soon wrinkled across their brow lines as they ran toward what they considered to be the exit zone. But their hearts would sink repeatedly as they kept encountering the same tree with the black mark! The anxiety that comes from being trapped in a maze clouded their consciousness, making them easy kill for Jose. They were dazed and confused and tired when he would creep close enough to attack them during their most vulnerable state of mind and collect his plunder.

As he divvies out his helpful tips to separate and conquer a village, Jose's devilish grin curls upward behind his moustache, and his fingertips tap against his cup as he looks through the 360-degree window from the lower deck of the ship. It perfectly frames the shoreline's stretching sands that seem to almost guide the crew's awaited return. Meanwhile, the other sailors pat Jose on the back, anxious to befriend the man that the king describes as the lion of the pack! The fragrance of fresh spice and the reflection of his face in freshly stolen, golden treasure cups send his body temperature north, while the boat winds to the west to ride the oncoming wave to dry land.

Suddenly, Jose clamors to his feet, winding up the staircase like a red ant hot on its trail! His anxious fingers glide over a row of 10 swords, as he narrows his eyelids and struggles to decipher through the haze of alcohol which blade was recently polished and edged-up against the granite boulder below deck. And as his fingers slip so softly, with a feather's graze, across the ninth sword, red proof trickles down his hand, serving as a liquefied testimony to which weapon would best coincide with his latest conquest. Beads of blood slowly bleed through a cut on his index finger, and he sucks it off as if it were mild pepper sauce in order to make sure that only the enemy's bloodline stains his swift sword. As the third-ranking captain in the Spanish army, the king sent him on a special mission to place their country on the forefront of the European map, adorning its legacy with bragging rights to what is referred to in modern times as Mexico. The soldiers were sent there to retrieve a surplus of jewels and stack-up on a slowly diminishing supply of salt stash, which can be located with the help of the Natives. Back home, these goods will surely sell out as quickly as a jug of water would in the Sahara Desert!

Meanwhile, Jose throws on his metallic armor and wobbles toward the edge of the deck, stumbling with his sword tucked tightly into its sheath. His head is still a little fogged from a fresh cup of cold wine, but he manages to grasp the wooden rail and stabilize himself against the inertia of the turning ship. Right before he steps onto the main deck, he exclaims to the crew, "Row with all your might!" and the sadistic memories of his past seem to just melt from his mind as his newest prey aligns with his eyesight. A new rush of adrenaline coats the effects of his dreary hangover.

He waves to the people on the shore that he visited many moons ago. The Native drums pound to greet their fare-skinned friends, accompanied by the shimmering beat of a pair of pearl-studded maracas. The music sharpens in clarity as Jose passes a set of trees in the distant shoreline, and the Natives lift their golden goblets up high, toasting their buddy's promised arrival. To return the gesture, Jose and his men all get on the main deck and extend their cups in a friendly manner.

But Captain Jose has been brewing up a wicked recipe, seasoned with trust and campfire cookouts. He and the native people have broken bread and eaten wild boar together in order to cultivate the principle of loyalty. He has told them many tales of how they will all work in harmony once the Spanish King stamps a fair price tag on the Indians' goods. And as expected, Captain Jose has returned, and the tribal people are awaiting a fair exchange for things they had given him like gold, jewels and so forth.

Jose's ship has almost decked onto the sandy surface. Celebration smoke mixed with spice pebbles rush back into his lungs. He blinks again and can visibly distinguish the lines and dimples on his old friends' faces. Clouds of euphoria begin to trickle down his memory bank as he recalls how the eyes of the Natives' wives glimmered when he had promised them that their husbands would be taught new trades and be able to enrich the common culture with new ways of cultivating the land, hunting for food on horses vs. barefoot, and they would also learn other ways of living from the land of Europe.

Jose was also known to hand out blankets to the Indians, which were secretly laced with latent spores of smallpox. Ahh…those were the nights when they'd all roast a slab of buffalo over an open brick fire together, swaying to the melody of the tribal songs. And some mornings, Jose got up at the crack of dawn to link arms with the chief and the rest of his people as they prayed. He wore necklaces crafted out of tropical flowers and clovers that can only be found in Mexico to prove he was embracing the new culture. These gifts were woven by the mothers of the village in celebration of their local, pre-teen boys' coming-of-age ceremonies. And as the boys vanished into the camouflaging patch of trees, Jose waited for them faithfully until nightfall so he could impose his common practice of the Tic-Tac-Tree game on the youngsters. Though he knew that he had killed some of the boys and sank their bodies in the river, he dedicated himself as a part of the search-rescue team to find them after they didn't return as expected from the coming-of-age nature trek.

He couldn't stand the small talk he was almost forced to engage in with the chief and his men, but the message from the king would eerily whistle between his ears: keep those people close so you can find out where they stash their goods! All of Europe had been watching Spain, wondering what the nation could possibly do to proclaim itself as strong. You must understand that these people had been downtrodden after centuries of domination by the Moors after they invaded Spain.

So Jose manipulated his way into the Indians' hearts to help his country, playing games of tag with the small kiddos, while keeping one eye on the whereabouts of the people who wore the most exquisite jewelry. During his first visit, his mind worked overtime to calculate how much time it took the Native people to travel from one dark burrow to another. But even when he retraced their steps at night to try and find their treasures, every cave he would seek out failed to produce the desired goods.

But the worst times came during the seasonal storms, as he would have to hold the nets as they all swam and hunted as a team. Jose would pinch his eyes shut and once submerged under water, he scanned the shallow bottom for any bump in the clay that could possibly serve as a hiding place for sunken treasure.

Seconds later, he would break through the skin of the sea like an angry bear. His eyebrows were slanted downward...he was so pissed off! As he dunked his head below the skin of the water to dig up the clay, all he'd ever come up with was a damn fistful of dirt and decomposed clam shells. After emerging from the currents of the sea, he was always seen with a look of disappointment. He would sit on the sand with his head in his hand, and the Mayans would gently rub his shoulder, telling him, "Don't fret now...your chance will come soon enough to catch the big fish!" They smiled while raising their spears. Jose's eyes would glimmer with humility and hide the true root of his disappointment:

not being able to find the damn treasure. Then it was almost as if a light bulb came on above his head as he conjured up a new lie that gave him a reason to depart and go back home, and then return once hunting season was over! After nightfall had dropped, he grabbed his signature grail and toasted to his newfound friends around the campfire after a tiring, muggy day.

The next day, as discussed, his crew dropped down the sails on the boat and let the currents lead the way back to Spain. Below deck, he massaged his temples, wondering what he was going to do. He was supposed to bring back the long-awaited treasure to the king! With empty treasure trunks, he was going to look like a mockery. Yet he chooses to wash away his worries by swimming in wallow and self-pity with his best friend, the faithful booze. Yet there's only enough for a ¼ cup of pleasure. And as he held his wooden cup while emerging back onto the top deck, he waved at the natives who became ever so distant as his men rowed away. Jose then climbs down the ladder attached to the exterior of the boat and takes his cup of distilled happiness and submerges it halfway underneath the skin of the tide water as the boat continues to sail away. Although the water dilutes the rest of the wine, it multiplies the volume inside the cup: a cheap solution meant to make him feel like he's got a full toast of happiness to wash the residue of worry from his brain.

After decking upon Spain's shoreline, he runs up the castle steps to the throne, wearing a fur coat equipped with ruby buttons. Pleading a thousand times, he begs his king's forgiveness for stepping foot in the castle empty-handed. But the king might have some type of compassion for him because Jose has always worked hard for him for many years, always producing the requested goods. But surprisingly, the king almost verbally castrates him for wasting so much funding. How dare he! The king gave him plenty of stock, drink and coined collateral to be able to take on such a trip. And he has the nerve to turn his pockets inside-out, lined with lint.

After a vicious verbal attack, Jose whimpers as he exits the silk-draped doorway, and it takes him months to recuperate from this royal humiliation and return to Mexico again to collect due payment. But with time, he finds his way back to the Mayan land, and we are back at the point of Jose's return. Anchors drop into the gulf coast, and as the ship gusts onto the beach, Jose's feet hit the sand as he extends his arm, firmly planting his right hand in the chief's grizzly grip. He later pulls out clay crucifixes to fit in the palm of all the villagers' hands. The center is adorned with a sparkling ruby, and its captivating luster lures the Mayan people into a deep well of fascination with gifts from their old friends.

Pulling them close into a heartfelt embrace, he tells all the people how he wants to show them how to make similar crafts, almost like keepsakes, so the Mayans can take them across the ocean if they choose to travel with him back to Spain. This way the men who are chosen to come along on the boat ride will have a travelling trinket, composed of elements from the homeland. The chief shows the cross to his wife, and she tilts her head roughly 20 degrees, but then perplexity turns into excitement. The skilled artistry is so fine and Jose is going to show them how to make gifts just like this! The chief's wife then asks her helpers to show Jose and his soldiers what else they have in-store that could be used to create such artistry. Now this may seem naïve, but in the Native culture, rubies, gold and gemstones are not hard to come across; they are as common as finding a dime on the floor. But the men still yearn to know where the Mayan piggy bank lies. So they plan to take the Spaniards into a cellar that is tucked underneath the webbed vines of the forest floor. Meanwhile, the foreigners' boots begin to sink into the snake-ridden dirt roughly half-a-foot up their legs.

A freight of emotions swirls as the Natives' stomachs jump in excitement due to their open hearts right now. The crowd's temperature festers with anticipation, which surpasses the humidity that weaves through the tree branches as they inch closer toward the underground entrance.

Suddenly, the men freeze like dry weeds while the wind continues to coast by. All five fat-bottom oaks are aligned in a pentagon shape, letting the Mayan soldiers know that they've entered Earth's purest axis, so they kneel in unison and pray, mumbling with lips that move 100 miles per minute.

Then, with each soldier placing his right hand upon the shoulder of the one crouched down in front of him, the group forms an elephant chain with each individual festering off the other's frequency levels. And in the foggy distance, the tip of the dawning pyramid pokes modestly above the mist to reflect sunlight toward the east. Remembering the positioning of the sun will help the men keep track of time. They then slowly rise and make way onto hallowed ground.

As the Native team grabs at the green weeds beneath them, a gray stone that weighs about as much as a car is slowly revealing itself as the men throw the leafy material toward the side to be carried off by the wind. Then the lead tribesman clutches a hold of the sun dial on top of it, turning it in a sequence to align it with a numeric formula, which allows a camouflaged entranceway to come forth. Suddenly a sidewalk worth of cement is seemingly elevated in midair as smoky vapors creep from its side panels. And it almost looks like the slab of pavement is being suspended purely by wishful thinking, as the chief and his men stare at the adorned wonder. The leader then gives Jose a pat on his back, and then extends his diamond-studded shaft toward the capsule, suggesting that this place holds paradise. The chief does this in a way that a buddy would when he's gonna show his pal the back entrance to the girls' locker room in high school.

As Jose edges toward the brink of this stone-etched portal, he takes a deep breath in and then follows the slippery, golden pathway to the point where the precious metals are being stored. The mist in the air heightens Jose's senses as they all go downstairs, and as Captain Jose sees a helper lowering the sides to close the gateway behind them, he jumbles the few phrases he knows in the tribal language to request that he leave it cracked to let in the cool temperature and fresh breathing air.

His trick works, and as Jose lowers his left eyebrow, he glances up to see that the men have propped small pegs underneath the stony slab to secure it from slamming shut. They get down to the base level, and then Jose quickly calls out an order and his men obey him without a whimper of hesitation, and then with bullets to the bodies, and a jab to the nose, almost 1/3 of the Native men fall down like freshly hedged weeds to face an untimely death.

The others struggle to get their poison-smeared spearheads out of their weaponry belts, but they can't seem to pull them out faster than the swift trigger of a firing gun. As bullets fly toward the broad target of brown skin, a pink mist permeates throughout the air, gently landing on top of the golden coins on the ground. The bloody sacrifice of the innocent treasure keepers seeps into the valuables. Sorrowful tears fall from a few blue eyes, but for the most part, the captain keeps a cold grin painted across his face, letting out a laugh as he celebrates his newest plunder. Jose then removes his leather-stitched hat and flips it over, and digging his hand into a bin full of blue diamonds, he pours them into his hat and then puts another palm worth of jewels close to his nostrils to take in the fresh fragrance of grim glory.

The boys climb back up the staircase to fetch some sacks and fill them up to appease the king's request. Feeling woozy from the mental exposure to a mass atrocity, they slowly trudge toward the streaking sunlight, as Jose's boot accidentally kicks the chief who is still shivering from the shock of his arm being sliced clear off. His eyes roll into the back of his head, as the feathers of his headdress vibrate against the floor. The man is choking on his own vomit! The dizziness of the whole situation causes the Spanish soldiers' stomachs to feel like loose, spoiled meat. Their vision is also blurred, mimicking the same sensation one gets from the aftermath of a venomous bite from a snake's cold kiss.

The truth is that in the deep core of this cellar, the circumference of the zoning area, plus the presence of the pyramid, births a radius aligned with Earth's energy levels at its core. This balances mini measurements of gold that detour any negative frequencies that could possibly pervert the balanced state of the hollowed cave. This also regulates the variation principle, promoting the suffocation of the allotted air supply to produce a precise composition of oxygen, as well as a mixture of other particles that are needed to properly sustain gold and other jewels.

The Natives have said for centuries that the power of the pyramid regulates any entry and exit by the composition of the soul and the value of one's karma. But Captain Jose is zoned out right now. He can't see or hear anything besides the sparkling effect of glistening gold that is piling up around him. And with some coins tumbling from the brim of his cradled shirt, he heads back up to the sunlight as the soldiers drop their heads and continue to hurry up the stairs.

Now most of the Indian's rose-colored sacrifice dried onto the surface of the coins, but it will soon be washed away from the precious plunder. The remainder of their blood is sponged up by the sturdy base of the stony surroundings, never to be forgotten.

Back on the banks, the Spanish sailors stuff cartons and containers to capacity with all they've just seized from their fallen "friends." And after gathering countless jewels, they lift their blood-stained swords toward the beauty of the stars, paying homage to the oh-so gracious heavens for blessing the purpose of this journey from Spain and protecting them.

Back home they do sail to warm milk from fresh, meadow cows, where their wives will surely unfold a stretching tablecloth before them. And of course they'll be generously rewarded for their tremendous accomplishments in the name of Spain. But the one who watches them prepare their ivory sails truly has the last laugh!

As the men reel the ship anchors back in, violins chirp in the background, and the mighty eye of Quetzalcoatl, the ancient pyramid guardian, watches the men whisk back to the familiarity of home. Back to the mainland they do sail, but all will be repaid in due time. See, you cannot fool with those who reside under the protective atmosphere of the ancient pyramid. If the ones you decide to raise a fist against have never made a mockery of you, then there will be hell to pay for it! If it's seen that you've harmed the balance of a civilization's peaceful existence, then pure havoc is destined to rain on the criminal's doorstep. In this case, it would be more enjoyable for the wrongdoer to opt out and stomach a full grail of arsenic than reap the power that the pyramid possesses to divvy out the criminal's crimson karma.

You watch. Just wait and see. The pyramid knows and sees all. Within its molecular composition, it bears a red line of pure love, which heads northbound, extending toward a plane directly above the ozone layer. But there's a thin line between love and hate, and this linear frequency can at times snake itself into a purple translucent ribbon of revenge, which embodies the inversion of peace.

The pyramid's frequency levels are also aligned with Uranus on a universal grid. Their levels intersect at the point where the rules of the universe's gaming program bend. This is the point where the zone can shift and align with the green axis of terror. In turn, this lime-colored zoning space is tied to a negative grid that falls in the sequence of -5, -4, all the way down to the perfect inverse of the number three. This is where the energy frequency from the pyramid can harmonize with the steaming wavelength that is constantly being released from Satan's ceiling. This is how the curse of the pyramid is allowed to reign down on those who harm the innocent.

CHAPTER Five

Crimson Karma

Meanwhile, Jose and his men are all packed up and the ship sails have minimized in the distance as the boat reaches what appears to be the edge of the stretching oceanfront. At this point, Vol. 1 of Michael's premiere past life has come to a close, and his spirit flips off the last page of this chapter, departing from ancient Mexico. His mind drifts back to the Chamber of Knowledge, allowing him to tie back in with his soulful self, which is still suspended in the cushiony movie seat. This chamber can also be referred to as Theatre #7 in the spirit realm.

As mind, body and soul are still meshing back together, Michael sits almost frozen in slow motion as he asks, "What, what's going on here, Dape! Am I back home yet?"

As he blinks his eyes, a humongous double-sided mirror is in full-focus. Supported by a silver stand, it begins to flip itself in a ghostly fashion, as a glow from the movie screen reflects upon the mirror's metallic composition. It just glows in a firefly fashion, somehow creating a foggy mist within the room.

Then, as the reflective ray makes its way through the atmosphere, it slowly ricochets from the flipping mirror onto a free-standing magnifying glass stationed in the southwest corner of the room. As the reflective ray seeps through the glass, it is allowed to pierce the irises of Michael's soul-self to create a point for vacancy. This extreme action would feel like a thousand stitches being ripped out all at once if he were on the physical plane. But Michael's soul is steady and at ease right now, and his earthly shell is in a dim daze, so he can't feel a thing.

Though the singe of the eyes may seem like an extreme measure, it is necessary because the heat cleanses, while broadening the windows of Michael's true self, his soul, and in a few minutes, he will be capable of acquiring the hidden talent of empathy beyond human control. This allows one to push beyond the pain and overcome distracting hurdles that come along with everyday life. Yet empathy serves as the soul's fuel injector as well, propelling one to overcome the effects of being downtrodden. This is a necessary tool when stationed on the mental frontlines of past life regression.

His body jolts as if he were awake, but this is merely an illusion, as his mind is still grasping to compress all this information. It itches for the opportunity to press play on a deeper past that has been long tucked away.

The theatre gets dark now. Michael's soul-self just sits there, with lightly burned pupils, waiting for a cue to find out what he is to do next. Dape's silhouette can softly be detected as she struts from the trenches of the corner, lowering her hands over his hollow eyes to gently close his fluttering eyelids.

"Michael…" she calls, as one would a cat to a small bowl of milk. But he pays her no mind; the bulk of his thoughts are still stuck in his past life as Captain Jose.

She claps her hands, saying, "Now this is very imperative, Michael. Please tell me what you *see*?"

His mind gains a subtle wave of consciousness and meshes with his spirit to form the jellied substance of a spiritual body, and not two seconds later, a beautiful, young, Native girl's soul emerges from the corner of the room. Her eyes puddle with tears, yet the lining underneath them packs away a flood worth of secrets. She's around the age of 12 or 13. She walks north as her eyes intermittently cut to the side of the spiritual chamber, making sure to take a mental picture of the trail of disintegrating flowers she is leaving behind. Yet each petal crumbles and burns as it comes in contact with the steamy, vaporizing floor. Her dress is laced with a bed of tiny rosebuds, each cotton-stitched by her mother. Yet it's obvious that she is lost and cannot find her way home.

"What has she lost, Michael? Do you remember her from the time when you lived as Jose?"

He tries to read the fine lines of worry streaming across her face, but her curious smile distracts him from solving her emotional puzzle. Yet all focus is instantly magnetized to the young lady's heart chakra, which seems to be the same color as the ruby dangling from her leather choker. The girl gently caresses the jewel, seeking some form of jaded comfort, but her heart still burns from the effects of depleted peace valves.

"Who is she, Michael?" Dape asks. Then emphasizing every word, she repeats, "*What does she want*?"

"I don't know! Um, I think she wants to tell me a story. Her lips are moving, but I can't hear any sound come out of them…ya know. Um, she's got some sort of backpack slung across her shoulder." Then a circular image is projected, overlapping the woman's presence, and the clip tells the story of how she used to live back in the olden days when she wrapped ears of corn in her dingy apron. Those were the days when she ran with fury toward the dusty sun to make it back home before dark. Michael reports what he's seeing in his mind's eye right now, and Dape tells him how the girl wants to repay him for something and she wonders what it is.

He turns back to glimpse the young maiden again, trying to figure it out. Wintry winds blow across her pre-teen face. In the ultra spiritual dimensions, seasons can be channeled and called to pass to represent the subject's mood. In this instance, the frost on her eyelids is representative of an eternal gloom. Snowflakes slowly melt across her lips as she mouths, "Pacheco!" And then her hologram disintegrates into a distant memory.

Michael lets Dape know that the gal must be lookin' for a man, and his name is Pacheco… it must be her husband or something. While turning to Dape for a nod of approval, to his dismay she shakes her head and extends her hand toward the main silver screen, and he notices a box of Mike and Ike candy that appears in his lap.

His shoulders are sunk back, but he follows her prompt and prepares his mood for another private screening. He dreads the storyline because nothing about that girl's vibe alluded to the fact that the upcoming flick might be a possible comedy or even a light-hearted drama. He takes a deep breath in and opens the box of candy upon nestling deeper in his seat. But as he breaks the seal and pulls the tab back, it reveals a hidden message: **No Just Means No.** Gently stroking the back of his neck, Dape caresses his shoulders and tells him to just relax as he slowly drifts into a realm of sleep. And as his spirit takes flight again, he prepares to slowly but surely arrive in the year 1542. Dape politely presses play to warm up the reels.

Michael then lifts his head again, and finds that he has joined the woman on a rocky, wooden platform, which is representative of another plane. He clearly sees the woman's face, but they are suspended in a room tuned to the range of slow motion. This same type of molecular speed can be found in parallel universes as well. The speed is written on a time track that is extremely warped by gravity, and that is why we as humans cannot see the physical manifestation of a parallel reality. Our eyes are trained to process the frequency of molecules at a steady speed.

This same type of slow motion effect is gently tied into the 3-D world as well. It is the hidden track that layers the composition of reality. This verse underlines Earth's atmosphere, harmonizing the ozone layer with the seemingly infinite realm of outer space. In a way, the dubbing of slow motion serves as the regulator.

Meanwhile, Mike's tender pupils are hollowed to the point of vacancy as the energy currents fester between his line of vision and the woman's dilated pupils. The two instantly lock magnetic eyesight as he involuntarily ejects his third self from his translucent shell. The element of slow motion allows the molecules of the spirit to be elongated and stretch across the sheet music of this hidden reality. This stalled pace of time allows the composition of the woman's soul to take on a stretchy effect as it solidifies, taking on the same effects of human flesh, and this temporarily lends the woman a sort of body for this project.

Michael's spirit then slowly situates itself down into her body. There it goes, disintegrating through her face as she breathes the rest of him in through her nostrils. The woman begins to shake violently as she is startled by the sudden spiritual transfer. The chemistry of her acquired body tries to regulate itself with Michael, who is composed of a foreign spiritual matter, and this doesn't make the process any easier.

There's no stopping the transformation. The grid of the galaxy is aligning perfectly behind the two, as the woman clutches her dark locks, yearning to hold onto a shred of control in some part of this vulgar reality. Michael positions himself all the way down to her feet as she straightens out her neck. As she tilts her head to the left, and then pops her neck, she rids herself of some pent up frustration. But her glowing eyes light up like a demon as she drops her head to examine herself from the bottom all the way to the top. She is now a he. The transformation is complete, and Michael now occupies her shell.

Right now, the woman's soul is temporarily absent from the body to make room for Michael, and its gloss-like composition rests gently above Michael's jellied body, which sits paralyzed upon the edge of the platform. With her head softly tilted downward, she appears to be asleep. She is done for the night, but Michael's task has just begun.

He yells out, "Dape, this is some twisted type of joke you're playin' on me here! Put me back in my body…I refuse to wear a vagina!"

He boldly grabs the crotch area of his dress as Dape enters through the trapdoor to smooth over the situation. "Relax, Michael, relax." She says. "I know how it feels…almost like your stomach is doing constant somersaults or something, right? But this is just because you're absorbing her past memories right now. You're still good ol' Mike, but to further purify your mind, your comfort level still needs to be stretched. This is nothing permanent, but you're about to personally witness the memory of her past!" He gulps as she lets him know that they're waiting for him on the other side. A twist of panic leaves an impression across the side of his face as he asks, "Who's waiting for me?"

And aiming at his skull, Dape shoots an electric current through her index finger and knocks him unconscious again, returning his soul to the spiritual portal of ancient Mexico to finish up the remainder of his very first past life regression. But this time he awakens on a bed of velvety snow, while in female skin. During the cold season, the forest reenergizes itself as all the flower seeds hide underneath the frozen soil, silently sowing themselves in preparation for a new spring. This is right before the moment in time when the Spaniards had set sail after slaughtering the tribe for their treasure.

His feminine voice cracks as he whispers, "Hello, is anybody out there? Can you hear me . . . God?"

Dropping to his knees, he repents toward the gray clouds for any sins, which he may have committed that brought him to this desperate point. Rattling off every transgression from either jealousy to lying, Michael runs out of delicate fingers to count the number of offenses he has accumulated. He fervently prays to be switched back to the form of good ol' Mike again, ya' know…sturdy and strong. But as he opens his regenerated eyes and stares south, he sees that he is still the proud owner of a juicy C-Cup. Rolling onto his side, he now tries to get up from praying but somehow he just feels too full like he ate two helpings of oatmeal. But he manages to at least pull himself up a little bit and posts his back against a mossy bedrock. And after lifting up his skirt, he slumps down to catch a glimpse of his belly, contemplating, *Hmm, so it's come to this? I'm now barefoot and pregnant . . . Jesus Christ!* He begins to mentally play out the commercials he remembers watching between chomping on some buttery popcorn and searching for the remote control. It was for the Plan B pill, and the lady looked so relieved after she had popped one with a smile. Somehow that girl in the commercial ended up making it out of the rain into the pharmaceutical aisle upon lowering the hood on her slicker. But there doesn't appear to be a convenient Walgreens in sight.

Mike panics and he's just not thinking right! He then fumbles for his phone…that will at least have Google Maps on it to find a nearby store or something. And once he grabs his mobile, he wipes the sweat from his brow, shaking the device at the sky, exclaiming, "Yeah…ain't nothin' comin' outta me tonight…Ya hear me???" But unfortunately, there's no reception right now.

"Silence!" replies a voice. Michael then dashes behind a berry bush and wonders, *What the hell was that?*

And as he trips over a grass-camouflaged rock, he lands flat on his stomach, but manages to pull himself back up by the might of a dangling tree branch.

"Well that's one good way to get rid of this thing," he says. As he rubs his back, he continues, "But next time, could you try not killing me in the process as well! Good ol' Surai, Dape, Mr. Rogers, Sesame Street and Friends, or whoever the hell forgot to RSVP for my personal hell tonight!"

"It's me!" hisses Surai, who is the dark one bearing the disguise of a jaguar. He emerges from the roots of the forest with the mark of the pyramid planted firmly upon his forehead. As a natural reaction, Mike kicks up dust as he takes off running, and his feminine booty bounces behind the skinny camouflage of a twig tree. Surai chuckles a bit, saliva dripping down from his jaw like a coyote, and then he leaps toward the tall weeds to charge at him.

Racing like a rabbit, Michael tries to reason with the guy, huffing and puffing, exclaiming, "Listen man, I know I might look pretty tasty right now, but . . ." And as he grabs one of his flopping breasts, he continues, "I ain't no good right now! I'm full of all that baby juice and nasty stuff like that…gives kinda a sour aftertaste, ya' know!"

But Surai pounces on top of his newest plunder anyway, knocking him clear onto his back, and the impact of the baby crashing against Michael's clay-like spine, sends souring shockwaves through his nervous system, pinching the very back of his eyeballs with pain. He steadily moans with more intensity than what comes with a debilitating contraction. Then, with a grim smile, Surai extends his sharp teeth like a piranha to intimidate his prey with their reflective glory. Steaming in the sea of uncertainty, Michael's pupils minimize with fear. The sun is going down, and no one is around to even bother to help him out. Chuckling with the glee that comes with the termination of yet another silly soul, Surai dives down toward Michael's neck, but in the nick of time, the pyramid vanishes from the would-be killer's third eye and converts itself into the reigning Spanish flag.

The beast's hour to collect another soul through direct feasting has just passed with the setting of the sun. Not to fear though. Sure, for Surai, it's always fun to kill those as their eyeballs bulge…sucking the fear out of a being is priceless, but it's already in the script that the little native girl that Mike's spirit now inhabits is in for the shock of a lifetime. As a result, the physical manifestation of Captain

Jose comes into crystallized focus, replacing Surai. Michael, who is still in the form of the young girl, is surrounded by a merciless fleet of men who lick their lips as they mischievously nod their heads and glimpse the young, native girl from hair follicle to toenail. These heathens can now finish off Surai's lingering deed. While clinching cigarettes with their teeth, Jose and his men chuckle, narrowing their eyes to further examine this young girl's busting cup size. He then motions for her to move her legs open by tapping her knee caps with the flat part of his sword, and then sways it to the left. Fear sizzles in the atmosphere, and Michael is unaware of what is going on with the shell he's occupying at the moment. His soft skin perspires as a natural reaction to extinguish a fearful victim's rising temperature, but it's not working, and Michael's ears pop, while sweat trickles from his temples, and the mind goes as blank as a fresh sheet of paper. As Mike attempts to plead for his own dignity, while intertwined with the girl's identity, he releases a vapor of a voice, begging for a drop of mercy this time and to simply pass him up. But sadly his cry is cancelled out by the communication barrier he has now assumed by becoming the indigenous young woman.

The captain then tells his crew to hurry up, and his men huddle, and their faces are partially painted with the silhouette of an early nightfall. They proceed to hogtie their newest plunder, and the rope chafes Michael's flesh until traces of pink soak into the rugged rope. Upon being dragged over jagged pebbles and trails of dirt, tears run down the victim's cheeks, as he wraps his hand around a vine that bears the girth of a hose. He tries to grab the ground to pull himself away from what feels like a murky fate, but his fistful of vines snap as the Spanish crew continues to carry him away. Within his mind, his internal scream bounces throughout his jagged brainwaves. In the meantime, he continues to reach for anything…a blade of grass, a claw worth of dirt, but it appears that nothing in sight is able to counteract the force of 15 sailors, and all he ends up doing is ripping his fingernails.

Still shivering with fright, Michael is inside a tent now, where violins, laughter, and tobacco smoke all heap the atmosphere. The shadows of drunken sailors devilishly dance against the tent's red fabric. But most of them have gathered around fireside to enjoy the unveiling of the newest prize!

Jose rips off the girl's ruby red choker, and then licks his fingers clean, tasting some raw flesh captured beneath his fingernails. Although Mike's soul, which currently resides within the young girl's body, had once possessed Jose's fleshly capsule on Earth, the script is allowed to play out without splitting Michael's soul between two human beings. This is due to the overlap on the time grid. Meanwhile, the rugged effects of Captain Jose's rape seriously tear apart the young girl's body, and even though Michael's soul has only been placed into the girl's retinal memory in order to feel first-hand what truly took place, it's almost too much for him to relive as his nervous system goes into shock.

While the woman's legs are twisted backward, salty tears burn inside Michael's heart. The pain and anguish of being penetrated in such a callous way causes the shame in his veins to break through and drown out his weary spirit.

As shock sets in, his eyelids flutter as if he were emerged in a state of seizure. Yet he is still able to glimpse the fact that Captain Jose was the first thief to commit the initial act of penetration. But not five minutes later, another sailor unbuttons his shirt with a daggered smirk, intending to relieve the captain of duty. The line of men just keeps growing while they all take turns and trade faces as if it were the night of Halloween. Michael still can't say a word, but the barely stitched seems of his heart continue to unravel as his mind bursts with pain until his soul passes out.

Half an hour after midnight, he manages to come to in a shallow pool of his own blood and notices that the men are all gone now, and the hazy air is quiet. His energy levels are low, and in a dazed line of vision, he sees three floating exits. But as he blinks his eyes, his sight quickly aligns and he's able to wipe away the hallucinations and realize that there's only one, single way out. He turns off of his back, plopping onto his stomach, planning to inch toward a clear exit way and seize the opportunity to make a getaway! Strangely enough, he can feel his own heartbeat as he could before, yet the constant thumping from the one of the baby isn't echoing through the lining of his belly anymore.

Yet in a race to save his own life, Michael continues to roll over in a flip-flop fashion as he keeps an eye-out for the return of his known captors. But the trauma of the extensive rape has chipped a small piece of spine out of place. Also, the girl's ebony locks are jagged and short. This is the result of Jose cutting a fistful of her hair so he can add it to his collection, composed of a white rabbit's foot and rare rocks from distant lands.

But the shame of not knowing who could have chopped off a lock of her hair to subtract from her equation of beauty rushes through Michael's whole aura as he bites his bottom lip to transfer the waves of extreme anxiety to a smaller place on his body.

While clinching his teeth, he then crawls across the floor on his belly and manages to grab the mildewed tent pole to pull himself upright, and a hot bank of blood begins to churn throughout his black and blue belly because it is time!

Pinching his eyes shut, he releases a warrior's cry and fluids jet through the torn birth canal as the woman's child plops into her cradled hands. Yet sadly there is no cry from the boy who was to be named Pacheco in honor of his father. The baby isn't breathing either. His eyes are still woven shut like a four-leaf clover's petals that never bloomed. It's apparent that the boy never awoke from his journey to Earth. Mama may have been strong enough to survive the attack, but the little baby boy's fading heartbeat gave out as the last sailor looped his brass belt buckle.

The rippling realization of death dawns on Michael, and his eyes dilate while they blacken like crystallized coal. As his guilty heart sinks within his chest, his soul retracts back into the Chamber of Knowledge. A bit of the truth has finally been learned. And his true karma was indeed returned.

CHAPTER Six

The Second Portal

His body jolts awake, and Michael slowly lifts his head as Dape proceeds to ask him, "Well Michael, how was it?"

Panting like an abused animal, his tone tunes to the pitch of confusion as he remarks, "How was what?"

She asks him if he enjoyed what he did over there years ago when he was the captain of his Spanish fleet. Meanwhile, all Michael can muster at the moment is a look of dumbfounded uncertainty.

While she shakes her box of Mike and Ike, which Michael had barely torn open before going on his journey, she peels off the message on the tab and hands it to him, explaining to him the precise reason why no simply means no.

She goes in-depth, telling him how on December 9th, 1542, when he was alive as Jose, he led a division of the Spanish army and proclaimed that all his men had his permission to collect whatever they wanted as a rightful reward, and a sum of all things included that young woman's child as well as her freedom to choose. Dape goes on to tell him that not only was the girl unable to have children after the attack, but she also subconsciously consumed the spirit of lust, which was exchanged during the sexual encounter she had survived. The spirit of lust destroys a life. She became infertile, and her then husband later left her and took to the side of a woman whose tender womb was still able to give him a son. This left the young maiden all alone with a strangely undeniable pelvic thirst for constant male companionship, a direct byproduct that comes when the spirit of lust chooses to inhabit a victim.

A roll of footage starts to project itself softly across the big screen, as the image of a nude Indian girl quivers with hormonal arousal. As the lusting spirit reaches maturity, the film shows how her narrow eyes cut quickly from the left to the right as she seduces countless partners. Her bare, moist lap chafes against a smorgasbord of men....sometimes three in a day! Her pigtails bounce up and down with a gust of excitement as if she were popping out of a 3-D animation book. She hisses and grinds her pelvis, while biting her bottom lip, with an unmistakable burst of satisfaction!

Licking the red residue from her trembling mouth, the taste of her own blood only further arouses this insatiable spirit. The spirit of lust always grows and festers unless it is cast out by town elders. But in this case, the girl never sought the help she needed. She just accepted that she had developed a high drive, and it must have come as she became a full-grown woman. As a result, the vibe of sexual exhilaration constantly illuminated across her face in the form of a girlish grin. The lusting spirit was in operation 24/7, not missing one day. And as the girl walked the village square, she eyed 10 men at a time as an excess of liquid steadily seeped from her vaginal opening. But in actuality, this lingering aroma of lust was not tied to her personality at all. It was merely the demonic spirit that chose to feast by operating through the girl's charmed body.

Dape pauses the clip, briefly clarifying the scene, while saying, "See Michael, when a child is molested, the spirit of lust is unknowingly transferred from the predator to the recipient and is allowed to incubate inside the human portal until it reaches full maturation in the house of the host." She takes out two cotton-stitched dolls. One is male, while the other is female. The male is bare-bodied, yet he has a little magnetized circle on him. The circle is composed of red fabric and has Velcro on the back of it. It is positioned near the male doll's navel in representation of the lusting spirit. As Dape moves him closer to the magnetized, freckle-faced, female doll, his belly button touches hers, and the red dot instantly latches onto her torso.

Although the male doll still has pieces of red lint speckled across his stomach, which symbolizes that he still bears the remnants of the lusting spirit, the actual magnet has since been transferred to the victim. So the spirit has been granted permission to live in a new bodily home and is stationed inside of the molested.

Michael puts his hand over his mouth as his face falls, and then Dape fast forwards the film to the section in the woman's life where she is in her early twenties and has since been banned from her native village and publicly crowned as the whore of the western woods. The woman slept with countless men and tore apart numerous households as she invited every other woman's husband inside her shack to share a sweet, passionate hour and a half that involved more than just a kind cup of coffee. Behind closed doors, the steam swirled throughout the house, and this wasn't just from a hot beverage. Her romp could be heard for hours as she quenched her undying, sexual thirst.

Fed up, the town women got the approval from the elders to invoke a public, distorted deliverance, which was disguised by the purity of ancient hymns and holy oil. In all honesty, the women wanted to humiliate this troll for messing with everyone's man. Their request was upheld, and the event occurred in the rainy forest. Soaking wet, the loose woman was crowned the whore as she mocked her attackers and got down on all fours, laughing at their sorry attempt to chastise her. The rain was coming down so hard that her brown nipples were visible through her thin, white dress. The townspeople also witnessed the fact that the girl deliberately didn't wear underwear that day.

The corners of her mouth cracked into a smile, while her eyes glowed with a blackened hue. She then shook her chest like a proud little canine, calling out the names of all the men whom she had been intimately involved with throughout the last week or so. Meanwhile, she further boasted her sexual successes as the angry village wives clutched corked bottles of holy water in-hand. The loose lady reminded all the women how big their men's penises were. She used both hands to illustrate the approximate length; casually throwing out helpful tips to satisfy their boys just a little bit better so the men wouldn't come knocking on her little whore-of-a-door throughout the star-studded nights! She then smiles at the ladies who repeatedly throw holy water across her back, casually telling them that she's got more helpful girlfriend advice if they'd like to hear it!

Out of complete disgust, one lady pulls up her ankle-length dress and kicks the woman right in the gut, and then pours a mini bottle of holy water in her mouth. The rightfully accused subject knocks the glass bottle out of the shrouded woman's hand, and then laughs like a child at play, throwing dirt in the winch's eyes, explaining how that wonderful holy water felt just like the sensation of her husband's bottled-up orgasm! Then the rest of the pack joins in by spitting in her eyes, and then rubbing blessed charms and earthly ash on her face to silence her boastful, whorish tales. Though her pride and body are scarred, as she cries on the inside, the spirit of lust gives her strength, and the whore of the western woods refuses to back down and silently agree that healthy sex is a sin! Within her realm of rationalization, she explains to the crowd that sin brings about grief, and if no one has bothered to notice, her sexed-up self seems to be the happiest one at this town meeting!

Though devastating, the young woman's relentless sexual rampage is not the true tragedy of the matter. It's the fact that her lusting spirit increasingly pushed her away from her heavenly placemat, and it did so even after her earthly passing. The sexual curse that came with lust lowered her energy frequency, sending her to the lower level right beneath the variations of heaven. This is the only place she could be allowed to enter in the afterlife. The heavens do not judge, but one can only enter the celestial realm that operates at a similar wattage as the individual's soul upon the time of death. This generates a magnetic match. And if a human being dies while his soul is still intertwined with a darker entity, at the time of passing, then the person will bear the same frequency level as the demonic spirit.

By that same token, the lady who was banned from the village did have a son, who as we know, died during childbirth. The spiritual eyes of the boy constantly watched his mother while she was alive on Earth. He always drifted along the clouded lining, which feels as soft to the touch as velvet shavings. He stared down at his mother from the mauve third ring of heaven, hoping that she might one day rise up in spirit and leave the frequency of lust behind her so she could join him in the afterlife on the crest of cool stars. This is the place where the hymn of the angels echoes against the springing walls. Yet the breach between the purity levels of the boy and his mother made it so there was no way her spiritual vibration was ever high enough so she could pass over and join him in the heightened level of the afterworld. As a result, there was a zero possibility for mother and child to ever be reunited.

It was the spirit of lust that was transferred from Jose and his men that drained the channels of the young woman's aura. In a pure and cleansed state, the woman's electric aura could harmonize and vibrate in the purest essence of purple and pink glory. Without the effects of the demon, she was naturally a very beautiful soul. Yet the trails of lust jaded her aura with a ghastly gray, which decayed her spiritual composition. In the end, this curved her destiny and prevented her from touching the coolness of heaven's harmonious gates. Before the time of the young woman's attack, she was an innocent girl of true purity, yet it was devoured through the torment of a pelvic sensation that could never be extinguished.

As the information is processed between Michael's earlobes and the stale movie clip soundly registers against his retina, he solemnly drops his head to Dape's side and begs her for some type of forgiveness because he never realized the type of agony he had unknowingly inflicted upon an innocent infant and his ailing mother…even if he did this in a past life. He repeatedly releases a melancholy melody worth of apologies, letting Dape know that he thought he was just doing his job as a loyal sailor!

Dape's eyes then widen with disbelief as she exclaims, "So you do remember some of your past lives…this changes some things, Michael!"

He confesses, "Well, uh…snapshots . . . little things, yeah. But not really anything in particular…ya know." He twiddles his thumbs and explains to her that he didn't even know what these open visions really meant. He just thought that his dreams didn't mean anything…just short, little pictures that glide across the memory in a state of sleep. He then adds, "To tell you the truth, I've always dreamed of a great, white pyramid, which stretched across an entire oceanfront. Actually, I usually see three of them. One is huge, the other is just regular, and then the small one grounds them all. They all descend from the great one that almost scrapes the sky! But it's almost like a small star is aligned with the really big one, which cuts through the dark blue sky. I mean it burns with such intensity, almost like its purpose is to ignite a fire within the tomb. It's breathtaking, truly breathtaking, Dape! And then the moon just dangles right above that star."

He wipes his eyes as his level of remorse seems to dry up as he recalls the vivid recollection of vanishing dreams.

And as he continues, he extends his hand to illustrate a picture of what he has been shown. He says, "I've always wanted to reach out and grab it to see if I could hang from that crescent moon or something, but my dream just won't let me in!

"There's almost like a hazy barricade within the dream, and it feels like some type of presence if I may say. It's invisible, but it gives off the vibe of omnipresence, indicating that there's a guardian who oversees the tomb. No matter how hard I push at the edges of the scene, or how much I scrape at the corners, I just can't get in!"

As he sits down, Michael pounds his fist against the arm of his movie chair, declaring, "And I wanna know who keeps me from this resting spot! I can almost swear to you, Dape, that somehow it feels like I'm supposed to be allowed inside…like it was designed for me way back in time. I know it sounds crazy, but I have to know why I always visualize a beautiful gray sea, lined with crystal pyramids, but right when I'm about to deck shore to come in, the picture fades away. And as the image is about to disintegrate, I continue to pull at the seams, and I'm willing to do anything just to get a peek inside, but access is always denied!"

He looks up and can see a devilish grin aglow on Dape's angry face. Since Michael has been gifted with a hereditary inclination toward intuition since birth, it's now apparent that his deceased ancestors must have been revealing hidden truths of his past lives to him before embarking upon this past life regression session. Dape now realizes that his ancestors who have crossed over must have been giving him clues, lacing his path with bits of premonition, to speed up the game plan so he can get closer to the room that houses the karma, the sacred city of Kullah. The presence of rage instantly nails a lightning rod through Dape's chest because this minor detail was not factored into the game!

Yet the good thing here is that Michael has bravely journeyed through his premiere past life as a Spanish captain, which has ridden his inner self from the spiritual bondage of lust. By experiencing the young girl's traumatizing rape, a piece of his debt has been reconciled, granting him access to the second voyage through the waves of existence to encounter the next past life.

But in light of this new information, things have definitely changed. Yes, he cancelled out a fraction of his accumulated karma, but Dape callously clears her throat and then points to the floor, asking Michael to look underneath his chair. As he does so, his hand reemerges, holding a leather rule book. And between intermittent coughs, he blows away a dusty blanket of time from its cover as Dape prompts him to read the second verse on page 12. Upon this brief review, the text reveals to him that outside coaching, without the blessing of the instructor, is strictly prohibited. And as a direct result, his voyage must instantly be recalculated. Dape programs the remote control, and Michael is then fast forwarded to a new level of spiritual review without further weaning.

His chair rapidly reclines, and hidden railroad tracks emerge from the floor as eight mini wheels drop down from the bottom of his seat. The carriage takes off, and then jets of light just pass him by as his seat interlocks with the track and speeds through multiple segments in time. These clips of history range from bath time as a small boy, to his first game when he swung that chipped up baseball bat at his little league tournament and scored a homerun for the whole crowd. Then his seat shifts onto a new steel track.

Sparks flying off this swiveling, metal course, the movie seat automatically makes a right turn at the merging segment in time as the molecular composition of this darkened, dimensional theatre breaks down. The grid of time then comes into full focus, encompassing our dear friend, Michael. Suddenly, he feels like an ant staring at a live motion picture as clips continue to pass him by, showing him how the ancient Romans would march in a sea of thousands. And with their silver shields lifted high, it was as if they orchestrated a reflective sea of spears as they trot toward their rivals. Michael rubs his chin in a mood of marvel, and the reel keeps rolling to the very tail end, and right when the last three frames are about to sync with the last three centuries, which have been imprinted on this universal tape, the surround sound picture box manages to make its image less grainy, and Michael's chair further reclines while the windy currents cut by his face. Yet the velocity of the ride drops in resistance to the oncoming winds. As he rubs his frosty hands together, he gazes through the translucent Saran wrap coating that separates him from the twinkling stars. Then, slowly, the protective film preserving the next scene pulls away as he approaches the season when the smoke of incense used to soar from the ancient Egyptian night sky.

The coach ride completely comes to a halt, and a pair of Aladdin-styled slippers sits outside his carriage on the granulated, desert floor. He hesitantly puts them on and then treks across the sandy surface to embark upon his newest journey. The last time he dressed this outlandishly was the night of Halloween when he got on stage as MC Hammer and sang a spoof cover of "Can't Touch This" for the crowd! But that night, he got paid major bucks to look like a fool for all!

Repeatedly blinking his eyes inside a now dry, ancient dimension, Michael tries to take in an unforeseen future, and he can't help but think that he sure wishes he hadn't let the cat out of the bag, alluding to the prior knowledge of his past lives. Everything could have been good if he had just sipped the Coke and enjoyed the damn Mike and Ike and not told Dape anything. But no...now he's dressed like he just got done smokin' a hookah with the Taliban! He rubs his eyes and they are still kind of sore from the last time they were used to do a spiritual transportation, and his veins itch with the rash associated with the HIV virus. They itch badly, but there's no Preparation H in sight. He wonders why it didn't dawn on Dape to even consider giving him a care package for these arising health conditions. But oh well...at least he's gettin' closer to the purpose of the cause!

All of a sudden, intermittent volts of electricity...no longer in length than worm bait begin to cluster about three feet ahead of Michael, and as they steadily compress and then expand, the wattage gets stronger in a glowing sense. He can't see the energy moving, but its rippling effects roll across his tight torso. The electricity is just a physical manifestation of the presence of the unknown. But as enough of it increases in volume, the picture slowly begins to piece itself together. A vertical, neon light forms to his left, while the combustion of the electric vibration slowly broadcasts an identical glow to the right of him. Red then illuminates on both sides of Michael. Yet Michael just can't figure out what he should do with this radiating set of parallel lines. Not 20 seconds later, a glowing, horizontal light flickers first on, and then off, as small sparks fizzle from its endpoints. It fails to come into full focus, until its bright, white counterpart begins to streak directly above it. All of the amazement of this supernatural event cannot be taken in with just one glimpse as Michael widens his eyes to make sure that his peripheral focus can capture what all is in store. With his heart surging like an unblocked water pump, he hears a knocking noise from the other side of what appears to be a door, which has been composed of the glowing lines of light. Yet there isn't a way to open it just yet.

His breaths of carbon dioxide escape his mouth at an irregular pace as an orange dot appears to the left side of this vertically positioned rectangle. It is suspended ¾ of the way down. It then moves a tad bit upward, curving to the left in a circular fashion, leaving a colorful trail behind, until what looks like a mini target comes into clear focus.

Michael's left eyebrow falls a bit as he tries to calculate what in the hell is taking place right now. As the target's sun-colored lines begin to bleed, filling in the width between the blank stripes of the target, the circular figure colors itself into one solid shade, creating a doorknob. But he still feels confused because it appears to be one-dimensional in nature, so it couldn't really lead anywhere...could it?

Yet the continued tapping from the other side eerily echoes, so he continues to pace across the desert floor, until he stands directly in front of the portal. The doorknob then glows into existence almost like a bright sign that says OPEN at a gas station. As he pulls his hand out of his pocket, perspiration beads coat his fingers, making it extremely difficult to get a firm grip on the little orange knob. But with persistence, the handle's cool-to-the-touch temperature sends a signal to his brain to cut off the waterworks and stop sweating. He wipes his hand on his pant leg with the intent to try again, and this time the knob clicks to the right, and he's given access to a new fortune untold. Visually, the door was one-dimensional and didn't look like it was even thick enough to house a few sheets of notebook paper, but Michael steps through it to enter the other side. He still has a type of three-dimensional body, but it has a different chemistry this time to help him endure the new elements.

See this place is a star gate to the distant past. You still have height, depth and width, but elements like oxygen are no longer useful since this level passes through a separate track in time. Here, plants and people no longer "live" per se. They are kept intact in the sheets of time so the elements that drive life, like oxygen, are no longer present in the realm of the past; therefore, the glistening streams of water have a gel-like texture to them. Currents no longer run with the rage and fury that prevail when oxygen marries her husband, hydrogen. All appears to be calm and still in the capsule of the past.

In this dimension, the images of time sit still like scenes on a cartoon strip, almost as if an animated rubberstamp came plummeting down in a cool, slightly wet little box of clay. In reality, a compilation of one-hundred little pictures crafts one cluster worth of a scene. And there the paused movie of the past sits…just suspended in time until a man from a latter day meshes with this particular portal to press play. Yet somehow the clip will start for a few seconds, and then stop.

Waves of color make their way up the rest of Michael's body as he decides to follow the sweet fragrance of distilled daffodils. The intermittent impact of a new human presence makes waves across the grid of the past, travelling like bending sun rays. And upon all this sweet, still glory, where the buzzing of bees blends with the beautiful bells in the distance, Michael can't help but be slightly bothered by the constant itching of his skin. He knows that sand is steadily depleting in the universe's hourglass, reminding him that the virus is starting to take effect now. And even though he has just arrived in the past, every attack from the physical, such as the HIV virus, or anything connected to mind, body, spirit, is now felt with twice the intensity.

Yet in regards to this galaxy, the present is somewhere within the framework of the zone of neutral. It's not at zero, because absolute rest is only achieved in the afterlife. But on a number line, the current frame of time is falling somewhere within the bracket of 2 or 3. Now when it comes to the future, the laws of physics must respond to whole and positive numbers, which constantly rip through the algebraic composition of time.

The indentation of the past sits somewhere in the negative scheme of time. Therefore when one first encounters the atmosphere of the past, peaceful vibrations first penetrate the pores, but this is just an illusion because it's so far back on the number line that it is able to mimic the positive components of peace, which are usually associated with the numbers of the future.

The future also has a vibration that is constantly moving due to its energy currents, composed of bustling positivity. Yet the past and the future were meant to balance the time track of the present to constantly keep the time of NOW in a positive course of action and follow the track of the future. The effects of destiny double when one fast forwards into the friction of the future; therefore, a form of balance must occur on the opposite side of the number scale as well. So as Michael travels deeper into the past, the effects of the poisonous brew gain potency inside his veins. The virus is rapidly festering inside his blood flow as it pushes toward the surface of his skin, serving as the culprit of his bothersome itch.

And as he walks toward a mirage of a constantly flowing waterfall, he sees a pair of conjoined twins broadcasted on top of its reflective surface. These boys are bonded at the head to symbolize their forced closeness. Kicking and screaming, they wail and squirm in an attempt to evade one another, but there's no breaking away from one's duplicate self. As Michael watches this scenario play out, he kneels down to get a better glimpse of what's going on. And as he does so, his heart chakra begins to bloom, generating pure, pale silver light, which sprays from his hidden core. The illumination projects itself onto the running stream, drafting a hollow bridge between Michael and the ghostly reflection of the twins. This is the moment when his soul is channeled into the twins' distant spirits through a narrow tear in the rhythm of time.

CHAPTER Seven

Justifiable Deception

Ancient Egypt. The Royal Throne Room.

Michael's spirit begins to mesh with a new scene and pearl-beaded satin sheets, the color of aged white sage, swaddle a shimmering queen named Natouja inside a sand-colored castle. She's smart…has the wit of Wiseman Solomon, but her jeweled crown weighs heavy on her brow line as she is faced with a decision that'll surely sway the course of the kingdom. She is now halfway dilated. Gripping her sheets with her fingernails, pearls pop off the embroidery in a sporadic sequence. Tears wash down her face in agony as the midwife holds the balls of her feet and insists that she keep on pushing. But the queen's foot slips through the lady's interlocked grip and hits her clear in the eye socket. With her head bowed down, a flash of lights flush throughout the maiden's left line of vision. And as the girl wallows in pain, Natouja doesn't even look her way and acknowledge that she just delivered a blow to the woman's face.

With fast-thinking, a fellow servant rushes to grab a hot rag and gently pats the girl's face. Meanwhile, the queen demands that the girls stay focused to deliver this baby tonight. The ailing midwife assumes a professional tone and immediately orders for fresh, hot suede towels to be bundled against Natouja's back, but the girl's throbbing eye begins to swell, preventing her from being able to lend a helping hand. Yet feeling a bit maternal right now, Natouja decides to be kind this morning and lets the young girl go home early…just today… of course without pay though.

The girl lifts her head in a wave of shock, yet chooses to silence her need for sympathy, obliging with Natouja's royal request. As the battered girl grabs her sack and heads out, the ambiance that the queen craves right now slowly creeps back into the room. Natouja lacks an emotional chip, and she subconsciously pushes away anything that may require sympathy or compassion. Searching for an internal refuge of peace, the queen inhales a cloud of myrrh, and then blows it back out into the air, snapping her fingers to make it known that it is now okay to proceed with massaging her temples. Another contraction surges right below her belly button as an undetected twin sways in his mother's stomach. Yet in the spiritual realm, more is festering than what meets the eye right now.

In the script of life, it is written that the firstborn shall be called Ishom, who is representative of Michael in his Egyptian past life. His spirit is as sweet as a blooming lotus, and he is loyal by nature. His halo has the inscription for obedience to heavenly laws; therefore, he would be perfect to promote justice and peace throughout the kingdom with the rod of righteousness! The other boy in Natouja's stomach bears the spiritual title of Alibabah, and he sees no real purpose to emerge in a land that's already been tilled and sown for his brother.

For it is Egyptian law: If royal twin boys are born into the same household, the one who the sun chooses to kiss first inherits the entire land. And the other simply becomes his brother's keeper.

Yet it was discussed last night in the spirit realm that although Alibabah will not be the firstborn, his journey is not going to be completely in vain. The brothers' spirits recently met with the gods as the angels stood there silently in the spiritual cradle of Kullah as the two negotiated a more favorable future, which could appease them both. Alibabah proposed that he give his first breath as a sacrifice to the gods. That way he could later be reincarnated as Ishom's son, and they could possibly rule separately in their own right.

He wrote this idea down on a 3x3 scrap of scroll paper as he stepped across the spiritual, jelly consistency that stretched out and served as the floor. He then folded the note as he stuffed it into the wishing box. Or so it appeared as though it was being placed inside the wishing box. In actuality, he held onto it so the writing on the paper would not register with the universal pull to grant the wish. And as he turned around to give his sibling a brotherly embrace, he placed the paper in his left pocket and walked through the pale, white exit door with the intention to become a physical manifestation upon the earthly plane. Now the rule is that if you write down the promise, but do not cast it into the manifestation vault, it goes null and void in the spirit realm because it didn't get the chance to consecrate overnight and turn to sap with the condensation of destiny.

Meanwhile, back on the earth plane, Queen Natouja is still struggling to birth her firstborn, and it almost feels like he's stuck, refusing to come out. Bubbles surge from the crest right above her pubic point, travelling up the belly button, and then they dissolve right before bypassing her throat. Although this feels kind of weird, Natouja just calls for more support to get the task done. Her maids work harder, and then the head missus of the palace can see the crown of the son poking through, so she reaches forth and gently swaddles him in the cradle of her arms as he is pulled away from the security of his ma's tender womb. As the maiden wipes the pink jelly from his sapphire eyes, she smacks his bottom, but the boy doesn't cry.

Yet with the spiritual eye, one can see that this is not Ishom at all. The switch of fate that Alibabah deceitfully initiated in the spirit realm made it so he was allowed to come out first. So to produce a diversion, he passes out, and lies motionlessly beside his mother on top of the sheets.

The midwives dash toward the boy, hoping to revive his fragile body with christened water and devout prayer. And as they chant with intensity, evidence of the ladies' change in temperature becomes apparent with their heating faces, which blush to the color of roses. As their level of faith pops and the waves of prophecy are emitted into the atmosphere, the electric static of their prayers is able to reach the hidden daystars. Gusts of wind continue to blow back the sheets on the bed, yet signs of life are still not present in the boy, and the maidens dread that his spirit may be gone indeed.

Natouja looks to her side and tries to poke her little guy, but still…no motion. She then shakes her fists in fear of what the angels of ash may have ripped away from her far too soon. But in the spirit realm, something else is stirring up.

Within the minute, darkly draped death warrens descend through the ceiling. These beings live on the third plane, the one that the human eye isn't trained to properly detect because the molecules cannot register with the current effects of human brain sensory. The beings' muscles are edified by the drapery of their hooded robes as they bulge forth. Although the average person cannot see them, their focus and intent send ripples of energy throughout the atmosphere. Natouja touches her belly, and she doesn't necessarily feel physically sick, but she can definitely pick up on a stench that lurks in the air. Her intuition tells her that something just isn't right here. But her maidens chuck up her bad mood to the early signs of grief from losing her dear boy.

Meanwhile, the warrens have arrived to collect their promised sacrifice. Although he tried to bend the rules of the game, the warrens are not easily fooled by Alibabah's attempt to cheat death to continue to live on Earth. They still intend to sweep up this cheater's soul before he gets away. As a kneejerk reaction, Alibabah's menacing spirit quickly regains consciousness, and as he tries to turn himself over, he cries as he realizes his newborn body isn't physically strong enough to quickly maneuver and run away from the dark ones. He thought this would be easy, but his heart is sinking with despair. So he uses the power of intention to detach his spirit from his body. This totally dissolves the earthly veil from his third eye, spraying violet rays across the room to distract his soon-to-be captors.

But the death warrens are also able to tap into the power of intention, sending vibes so strong from the unblocked channels of their minds, creating a shield to interrupt the oncoming sensory waves of a distraction. An invisible form of glass instantly blocks the magnetic waves from Alibabah. And as the warrens kick up dust, they steadily move in for the kill. Yet they still proceed with caution, given the fact that this little devil is pretty powerful. All the teachings conducted by the gods have been preserved inside the mind of the two twins. Yet Alibabah is without his wingman, Ishom, and is all alone right now. Therefore, he only possesses part of the power that is required to access all the answers to pummel oncoming forces.

All within a spiritually conscious state understand how powerful these two brothers will become if they are allowed to reunite. Alibabah has already proven himself to be deceptive; therefore, he must be stopped at once. Yet there's one minor detail to consider: Alibabah now lacks a body. That is one plus for the death warrens because he cannot directly carry out malice on Earth, but to further sabotage him, Alibabah must be returned at once!

The violet vibration level in the room soon transforms into an abyss of violent waves. In the wave of sound that is sharpened to the point beyond human interpretation, it sounds like a steaming train. So the warrens cover their ears and struggle to stay focused while gusting winds rip free.

Meanwhile, Ishom is now ready to pass through his mother's birth canal. A twist of surprise scurries across Natouja's face in disbelief as she realizes that she was carrying twins and is going to be given a second chance to be a real mom! As Ishom emerges, the boy's gurgle is intertwined with a childish giggle as he greets the sunlight and takes in his very first human breath. Then, slowly, a red glow radiates from the left side of Ishom's skull. It marks his identity and can only be viewed in the spiritual realm. Alibabah catches the signal and slowly lurks close.

As Alibabah's third eye identifies Ishom's aura from across the room, death's helpers are blindsided by the beaming lights engulfing the two twins. But they soon wipe their dusty eyes to realize that it's already too late! The boys' purple and crimson auras have united as one, painting the maroon vision of victory against the palace walls. The nemesis has formed, and the brothers' energy fields can in a way rule as one.

Egypt's sure got its work cut out because according to the blueprints of history, this is the very moment when Earth's core first began to crumble. Although Alibabah managed to escape the grip of the characters that mimic the persona of the grim reaper, this small turn of deceit and mischief communicated a fracture as thick as a baby's strand of hair somewhere in the layers of time. In this case, a debt still must be repaid in order to regroup a sense of balance within the universe. Although Alibabah managed to make it through and can now thrive off his brother's energy field, the tallest death warren shakes his finger at the boy as the sands of hell fall from it, marking him for a future of damnation on Earth.

Queen Natouja howls to the maidens, "Where's my child?" A lady then hands her the one surviving son as she removes the swaddle draped over his face, which gives way for the glow of the maroon mark of the pyramid. It is only visible from a spiritual standpoint, but it is definitely in the middle of the boy's forehead. It pulsates much like a bleeding heart. Meanwhile, Ishom chuckles as he looks up at Alibabah's spirit because he's the only person who can see him on Earth. Alibabah chuckles, too, with the eyes of a serpent. Alibabah's spiritual wavelength, a.k.a. the mind, has securely latched itself onto Ishom's aura via a translucent, purple string. He now has all the frequency he'll need to thrive on Earth.

Though he is invisible to all others, Alibabah has the help of his brother Ishom right now and that's all he needs. The passion to live caused him to conquer the unthinkable: Sure Death. And passion is a very, very blessed thing, especially when it comes from the sacredness of a mother's heart. But what happens when her love begins to send mixed signals?

CHAPTER Eight

Wrongfully Accused

Many years have passed since the twins entered the veiled texture of the earth realm, and Ishom, now fifteen-years-old, watches a purple tree sway in a sun-soaked vase on top of the kitchen counter. But he dares not give it a touch for he knows that the instant gratification of his senses could never cancel out the pain of his mother's harsh scowl. Suddenly, a familiar purple aura rushes across the side of his cheek, and as he trembles, staring down at his shoes, he realizes that he is no longer alone.

"Do it," says a spirit.

"No, Ali, I won't!" replies Ishom.

The menacing voice of Alibabah then announces that he'll carry out the deed instead. As Alibabah uses the potent power of intention, the vase gently wobbles in a circular motion on the table. First slowly, and then faster and faster!

Ishom warns Alibabah to stop before he gets him cussed out again, and then a ghostly image of Alibabah's face unveils itself to give a glare of disappointment. He can't believe that his brother doesn't trust him anymore.

As his soul is still intertwined with Ishom's mind, Alibabah gathers his electronic senses, generated by the synapses of the brain, to transfer a charge from the spiritual brink to the physical plane. The energy waves counteract with one another, positive first cancelling out negative, until a simple, harmonious wave of energy is brought about into existence, meant to knock over the vase on the table.

With a switch in-hand, one of the caregivers darts down the hall and demands a reasonable answer from Ishom as to why his mother's favorite piece of artwork is crushed into one-hundred tiny pieces on the floor.

But before she can even finish her familiar scolding session, shockwaves invade her pores in light of what Ishom just did! The jasmines are spread neatly about the black and white checkered floor as their aged buds desperately lose vibrancy. The maiden knows that the queen's flowers will surely die if she doesn't do something quick! Out of fear that she won't be able to resuscitate the ailing buds later, the maiden lifts her gown, pops a squat, and releases a human flow of urine to replenish the seeds. Although this act would disgust many others, the maiden's quick wit will most certainly be understood by all who know how much the queen adores her darling little flowers. Natouja's fervent meditation, while in the presence of the flowers, can sometimes persist for hours.

As the last drop trickles down the side of the woman's leg, she turns to Prince Ishom, grabs his arm firmly, and then proceeds to ask him why he was playing around with the jasmines in the first place...he knows how special they are! Ishom is shocked and he wonders if another beating is on its way for something he didn't even do. Yet as always, he simply points at Alibabah's invisible soul in front of him and refers to his deceased brother. Rolling her eyes, the maiden immediately escorts him to his mother, Queen Natouja.

As Natouja bathes in the rhythm of the sun, she sips her fourth glass of fig wine, while her servants fan her, and they hardly stop at any intervals or bother to even think to request a sip of water. But still she is dissatisfied. The queen's unpredictable temper begins to accelerate, aligning with the heat waves of the sour Egyptian sun.

Slanting her gray eyes in discontent, she softly sighs in sight of her son, knowing that Ishom must've fudged up again this time, and she raises her hand to cease fanning.

The maiden bows her head in a moment of silence until given the cue from the queen that it is okay to speak in her presence. She starts out saying, "Dear Queen…I'm sorry but your jasmines..." And at the tail end of the woman's sentence, Natouja yanks the fan's peacock handle away from a servant, swatting Ishom right across his neck, and he trips over his own sandals in an attempt to escape a second sting.

He cradles his neck, crying, swearing up and down that it really wasn't him this time! As another string of pride splits within his heart, he stomps his unbuckled shoes out of sheer frustration, and the simple fact that Ishom has enough guts to mutter his dead brother's name again in his mother's presence starts her out on another rambling rampage.

She hisses, "Listen to me! I will not tolerate such foolishness coming from a man who is to be crowned king. Ooh, if only your brother had survived, I swear I would've spewed to the world that he was the firstborn! A dead man would have more common sense than you sometimes!"

Tears flood beyond the lining of Ishom's eyes. As the whipping words of his mother tear whelps into his spiritual self, he plugs his ears and wishes that he knew how to combat such a sense of negativity that won't stop flowing toward his direction. But without the seeds of wisdom planted by a father, or the comforting confidence that can be instilled by a mother's nurturing words, he wilts in a deep pool of self-pity as his mother howls, "Oh don't you give me that look! You've been behaving like a mad man ever since you've been able to talk, mumbling, 'Here he comes, my dead brother, flying over my bed.' Or, 'There he goes, winking at me through the trees again!'"

Knowing that the tone of one's voice is able to drum home the seriousness of a verdict, Natouja drops her pitch to the vibration of a deep gong. Hatefully smiling, she throws her drink at his feet, sneering, "*Pit-i-ful*...I dreamed of so much more for Egypt!"

Natouja then turns her body toward the east in hope that somehow the translucent sunrays will absorb her mellowed misery as she beckons for a refill of liquefied joy.

Hunched over like a weeping willow, Ishom shamefully drags his feet upstairs to retire in his room. Now most of the time when Mom goes off, his heart simply feels overly exposed like the hollow wind could blow right by his rib cage, rotting his heart with chill. But this time, it was almost as if ¼ of his main organ had been slowly pulled out of place and not properly bandaged with the tender caress of love. And every time Natouja opens her mouth to slash at his heart, it steadily decays his soul with the woe of emptiness.

Once behind closed doors, Alibabah's voice bounces off all four walls, telling his brother that he's all he's got!

But Ishom simply goes on to explain that Natouja is still their mother, and she's just trying to give him some advice so he can get better. He tells Alibabah how it must embarrass her when people see him talking to a so-called spirit at the dinner parties. Hell, his mom nearly slapped the meat tray clear out of his hand the last time he explained to their guest, the princess of the east, that his dead brother was sitting right next to him on the couch. Ishom really starts thinking about things and realizes that he mainly receives punishment when Alibabah engages him in small talk in front of people. He remembers how Natouja said that it looks loony, and then he bites his lip out of rage, telling Alibabah how this is all his fault!

"I understand how you're feeling, Ishom, I really do. But we were meant to be together, see..."

Alibabah then points to the thin, purple thread, which connects their minds, uniting them as one solid mass. He then proceeds by explaining how it was written in heaven that they were elected to be the chosen ones to rule over the desert sky, and how Natouja was just the carriage part of the deal to get them to the earth plane. Alibabah points to their connection point, causing Ishom's eyes to turn maroon as he locks spirits with his brother. Then Alibabah's image gives off the persona of Jafar, that evil thief from the movie Aladdin. Yet Ishom continues to give him grace and listens to his tales because, in the end, this is his brother who is bound to him by both blood and spirit. Alibabah then insists that he just bent the rules a little bit when he defied the death warrens. Ya know, it's the same way you would curl a water pipe to make the water run smoother. He explains that he had fixed the spiritual problem, but only for a short while. He then expands on the fact that he needs Ishom's help so they can harvest a hefty future together. Ishom shakes his head, and then picks up his nunchaku, a Bruce Lee type of weapon, reviewing the stances from his kung fu lessons. This is just to brush up and ignore any new form of manipulation that Alibabah might be trying to spew forth this time.

Alibabah's ghostly hologram boasts itself as he pokes his chest out and broadens the width of his shoulders. He moves his hands like a magician, creating a smoking screen upon his torso as the scene plays out.

It is then displayed how in the future, Ishom fastens the ruby clasp on his tiger skin shawl, and with a grand smile across his face, he steps to Father Pharaoh to accept his rightful place in the history of the kingdom. The short film evaporates, shifting focus back to Alibabah as he hesitantly admits, "Now Ishom…I know we haven't always agreed on everything, but if you listen to me, then you could succeed to the throne and we'd become the richest nation the Middle East has ever seen! And Natouja could finally vanish as you take your rightful place in the books of time as the king!"

Ishom squeezes his nunchaku, reminding Ali that he's already scheduled to take the throne…Ma and her maidens are just waiting on the right time for it to be announced. She and her maids have been bowing and crouching at the throne almost every other night to gain confidence on the matter…it's just takin' a little time to hear back from the Gods on when the time is right…that's all! Their prayers have been interceding between the clear, bendable veil that lies between Earth and the outer limits. Yet Ishom doesn't seem too sure of himself as he repeats his mother's excuse this time. As Alibabah playfully gives him a look of doubt, Ishom throws his kung fu weapon to the side to sit and bask in a sea of raging thoughts to really gain a perspective on the matter at-hand.

He rests his narrow chin in his hand as he gazes at Ishom with a smirk to let him know that he actually won't be getting anything at all in terms of the throne. Ishom's eyes swell up this time as he whines, exclaiming that his mother will keep her word and his time shall come to rule…Mama had promised him!

Yet Alibabah continues to deflate his brother's fragile balloon of faith, reminding him of the time when he was supposed to get an increase in his monthly allowance. That was supposed to happen last year, but he's still making Natouja's oatmeal every morning for free.

The memory of another broken promise simmers in his amygdala, the portion of the brain that processes anything that could possibly produce negative vibes. With Alibabah's spiritual eye, he notices how this section that processes Ishom's painful thoughts progressively paints itself from the ripe complexion of an orange to a raging red. Though his insides are twisting up like a coil of tangled cords, Ishom only blushes just a little bit, nodding his head, recalling all the times she broke her word to him. He constantly felt like a kid who was made a promise to visit the candy store, and then he daydreamed about all the different flavors of bubble gum as the corners of his mouth moistened with anticipation. Yet when he went to unwrap a piece of joy, there was nothing in there…just a bundled up joke strip that led him to have faulty faith in his mother's words. And just like a balloon that lost its air, his heart sank from one level to another until it just didn't have enough air to keep floating. Natouja's broken promises felt like a stinging sword that kept nicking at a section of his raw heart! Turning with droopy eyes of desperation, he's now ready to hear the rest of what Alibabah has to say.

With his first hook of manipulation now anchored into his brother's psyche, Alibabah then unrolls another movie spool, proceeding to reel him deeper into his web. In the spirit realm, Alibabah's third eye trembles as it shimmers into the complexion of maroon, projecting what appears to be a scene from a movie onto Ishom's dilated pupils. In the clip, Natouja is in the study speaking with Father Pharaoh to review some not so great details concerning Ishom's advancement.

She paces the marble floor, which is lined with Roman artistry. And with a drink clutched in-hand, she moans, "But Daddy, he's not a fit ruler, period! He fantasizes to himself all day long and embarrasses us in front of any company we have. He can't even finish one of his Kung Fu lessons without dropping out of stance, swearing up and down that his dead brother's spirit is blocking the view of his instructor; therefore, he cannot fully concentrate. He said he likes to do all his homework in the dark so he can't see the supposed ghost of Alibabah!"

Spit spews from her mouth with anger as she places the leather chains on her father's desk to assure him that he will be bound respectfully to receive a very quick death, with the capstone of a sudden twist to the neck. As the dark clouds bring forth a roaring sea of wind, she draws the blinds and then continues with her plan, expressing how her cousin Juaheem already agreed to drive him out to the Nile tomorrow night, where no one will be able to hear or see anything at all. He'll then be mounted on his horse, and they'll crack the animal's knee caps to make it look like he had hit a rocky patch in the road and the carriage turned over into the water banks. That way, it will be said that the whiplash of the accident broke Ishom's neck upon impact. Stroking his silver beard, Pharaoh hesitantly asks her who will be left to rule with him, and Natouja caresses the bottom part of her belly, gazing up at the snow white moon with a smile, reiterating the fact that she still bleeds moon by moon and could be with another child no later than the end of next year.

But during the absence of a male heir, she will humbly offer her services to assist Pharaoh by governing the throne as an understudy. With her hair flowing in the fresh winds of the twilight, Natouja's eyes sparkle with the glimmer of a small girl, as she nods at Pharaoh, sponging for any drop of approval that she can wring out of him.

Pharaoh is now weary with the effects of night sweats as he drops his head, lacking enough energy to even sigh this time. The tint of his hairline is beginning to match the silver locks of an aged fox, with a receding hairline that trails back to the beginning of his ears. Each year his hair seems to progressively move back about ¾ of an inch due to stress. Pharaoh's reservoir of hope continues to fade away as he recalls all the times when he had to bitterly watch Ishom release a pathetic swing during one of his kung fu lessons. The boy's report card always stayed the same whether he was graded in kicks, punches, jumps or warm-up exercises. The instructor's note always read: Potential. Think of that word…potential. What a miserable little word! The connotation is comparable to the concept of an athlete, who always reaches for the baton, and it is close, I mean it is right there! Its reflective, maroon glory magnifies in the sunlight, but it's always about 2 feet away. Sure, one has the **potential** to reach for it, but the fingertips don't quite grasp the illusive glory.

In the suite, Pharaoh finishes up recalling Ishom's failed plights, while turning his head toward his daughter. He can't help but notice the constant drinking of his frail sweetheart. First she started out with wine, and then things progressed to the clear liquor with the higher proof. She sips from her glass between sentences and appears to be rolling her eyes, but in actuality, she's just fighting to stay awake in the middle of the afternoon! He looks at his baby and can see the bones in her back poke through her flowing white nightgown. The sight of her deteriorating health only fuels his need to bring about a sudden conclusion that might somehow promote change in his household.

Rubbing her eyes, Natouja sleepily adds, "But this time when I have another baby, I won't mix my genes with Hassan...that way I can have a chance for a sane child! I know he is my cousin, but when Uncle Jerig married that queen of Persia, something didn't link up during the night of conception to produce something like Hassan."

Although incest is frowned upon today, it was a very common practice at this time to keep the royal bloodline pure. Natouja then drums her point home to make sure that Pharaoh doesn't order for her to be impregnated by him again, telling Pharaoh that something just wasn't right with him, and somehow there must've been a genetic glitch, which he passed down to Ishom.

She rushes to her daddy's side, uncontrollably pouring her tears into his lap, pleading to allow her to start over and try again just one more time. Pharaoh then caresses the side of Natouja's cheek, and breathing in deep, he softly nods and obliges to his ailing daughter's undying request.

Ishom loses eye contact with Alibabah, and the film then cuts short. He sits straight up on his bed and interlocks his fingers, simultaneously lowering his brow line, asking Alibabah how they plan to stop her before it's too late. Alibabah then crosses his arms, softly chuckling as he breaks into uncontrollable laughter. He then assures his dear brother that they'll be able to supersede her tonight!

CHAPTER Nine

Life After The Earthly Life

Night is falling, and the rays of the drifting sun seep into the pink desert sands as Alibabah leads the way. They're creeping into Natouja's secret cave underneath her pyramid, which was built to conserve her power during her passing days.

On the way down the hill, Ishom trips over a small rock and exclaims, "Hey…uh…Alibabah, do you think you might be able to look out for me next time? I mean let me know if I'm about to hit something. You're supposed to be the one with all this X-ray spirit vision!"

Alibabah jokes with him, stating the phrase: *I just can't do it captain!* And after the brothers laugh a bit, even though Alibabah's chuckle is unmistakably grim, Ishom simmers down into a more somber mood. But in all seriousness, Alibabah can't help but feel pain. He says that the anger that Natouja had two kids, decided to let one die, and then plotted to demolish the only one that she still had left is taking up the bulk of his thoughts right now. Although Alibabah does have a hidden stake in Ishom's rise to glory, he still can't help but feel that they both got slighted in the process.

As his body was vacant on the bed, his own mother didn't even bother to give him a proper burial. She didn't even prepare a bundle of sheets, soaked in fresh oils, incense and holy water, to drape over him while his tomb was erected. She pretty much told a silent lie as she announced Ishom as the only child to the people, not even bothering to say that his twin didn't make it through! Natouja wanted to avoid the shame associated with the image of infertility, or the idea of delivering a stillborn. In Egypt, this was not socially acceptable at that time.

But Alibabah is still baffled. Sure, she didn't want to tell anybody about his death, but he didn't even get a proper mummification…no prayers…no nothing. His body was simply discarded of in a straw basket along with rotting fish bones, empty containers and anything else that was titled as unwanted. Alibabah tells Ishom of the heartache that he's had to carry around all these years as he watched him receive the majority of the attention he yearned for. Sure, Ishom had his fair share of problems with Natouja, but at least he was properly dressed every morning by the servants, as well as protected by the guardsmen.

Ishom can suddenly empathize with his brother's pain and has no problem letting him in on his inheritance of the throne. This is to make up for all the lack he had to experience. But he gently asks Alibabah how he plans to rule over Egypt if he lacks a body. Alibabah appreciates the sincerity of his brother's concern, yet his eyes widen with greed when he declares that all he'll need to be allowed to rule is simple access to Natouja's spiritual tomb. So they continue to march like soldiers throughout the thick of the blanketing night.

Not much later, Alibabah comes to a screeching halt, and the hair on the back of Ishom's neck stands up as he feels a resistance in his brother's drive to continue. As Ishom turns around, his brother's voice slowly melts to sap. Meanwhile, clearing his throat, Alibabah makes the decision to confide in him about the fact that he still has a debt lingering in the spirit realm. It's in the outer limits, right between the daunting towers of existence.

Underneath the sleeves of his robe, Ishom clinches his fists, leaving the imprint of his fingernails in the palms of his sweaty hands. He fears what kind of crazy request could spew from his brother's mouth this time. And as Ali continues, he says, "Ishom, I ran from death during our birth, but I can't keep running anymore. They're hungry for a soul!"

Ishom can't help but wonder if he's gonna suggest that he give up his own life to cancel out the debt. Sure, he does feel some type of connection to his brother, but nothing would get him in the mood to kiss the eternal darkness of death for him. He sadly lets Alibabah know that there's no chance of self-sacrifice right now…sorry!

Though he is a bit shocked at the simple thought that his brother might say no to anything he requests, Alibabah shifts gears and points to Natouja's bedroom window, telling him to rest assure that if anyone will be losing a life tonight, it'll be her. He tells his brother that he's just gotta get the key to do it first.

Ishom scratches the back of his head and crazy thoughts flow throughout the inner lobes of his mind as he pales in sheer shock of the mere thought that they might be ending their own mother's life with the sharpness of a rusty key.

Shaking his fist at Alibabah, he scolds him, proclaiming, "Of all the mess you've gotten us into before, I swear I thought you were better than that . . .Alibabah! You wanna kill her with a key? Come on, now!"

The thought of family loyalty causes him to pull away from anything that could inflict perpetual discomfort upon her. But then he starts to flip through the open chapters in his mind, and in a couple of seconds, he remembers that he is the next course on the platter of death right now, courtesy of Mommy! Miraculously, his fists open back up into palms as he rummages through his pocket for a possible skeleton key of substantial length to execute fleshly penetration.

Laughing at his brother's remarkable change of heart, Alibabah strokes the ripples of Ishom's conscience, letting him know that it's not in the plan to kill anybody tonight. All they'll do is give the fragile queen a sort of a sleeping pill, that'll last for a century or two, through the use of her life key. Then the brothers will be able to rule as kings. His voice springs with bass as he reiterates, "Great kings!"

All Alibabah plans to do is occupy Natouja's body for a little bit, so he can rule in flesh form with Ishom. And then he'll use Natouja's royal powers to cast a witchy spell and bend Pharaoh's decision to have Ishom slain. While under the charm, Pharaoh will then be prompted to commence Ishom's early royal coronation.

Ishom likes what he hears from his wise brother. Alibabah is solely composed of a spiritual frequency and has been travelling through the wavelength of Earth's extended dimensions for years. Yet due to the weathering effects of time, his soul is constantly losing energy with every passing day, plus his combustion levels are constantly grounded by Earth's peppered gravitational fields. And if his soul passes through a strong enough pull, he is drained for the day and is so tired that he can't even see 10 feet ahead of him. At times, he sporadically leaves the bubble of the ether and comes up for relaxation in outer space. At least this way there is no gravity in space and he can build his levels back up before returning to Earth. But now, Alibabah is slowly losing the ability to channel himself as a spiritual presence on a heightened earth plane, and he can't keep living off the conjoined energy field that he shares with Ishom. Not only is he depleting Ishom's aura, but his soul has already sucked up the main force that stems from the brothers' electric bond, and the bank is running dry!

Alibabah points at the illuminated string between the two of them, and its once maroon tint is now depleting into a ghastly gray.

Tears flow from Alibabah's eyes as his hologram flickers in and out of focus. He tells Ishom, "Now Natouja is just breathin', eatin', taking up air and hoping to reproduce again one day when she's already been given two of the best men for the job! But she turned away from her true responsibility, so in my opinion, she brought this upon herself. And when we find her life key, we can temporarily dissolve her spirit into the vapors of existence, and then I'll gain control of her body…ya know!"

Ishom pulls a lamp out of his backpack, lighting it up while asking him to lead the way to her spirit volt. Barely guided by the reflection of the moon, Ishom lifts a trap door, buried by sand, and slithers down a creaky staircase underneath the pyramid. Alibabah closes his eyes, mentally scanning the cell until his third eye picks up hollowed vibrations, and their wavy patterns correspond with the heightened ringing, which echoes throughout the cave. As the sound bounces off the walls, the waves invert themselves, reaching the highest peak of any earthly pitch. Then Alibabah's vision turns snow white, like he just lost a TV signal during the super bowl. He points north, toward the ceiling, to let Ishom know that the force must be over there somewhere.

Barely grasping the crumbly boulders in the wall, he knows he won't be able to climb up that far. So he grabs the spinning ladder along the wall and pulls it close to him, and with cat-like curiosity, he finds himself almost 50 feet above the floor of the cave. He pants as the oxygen layers thin out, and sound increases with intensity. Continually being directed by Alibabah toward the main prize, he asks, "Am I close?" Alibabah lets him know that he's right where he needs to be…all he has to do is lift his right hand just a tad…there…there…that's it! Given the green light, Ishom reaches up to grab a two-inch tall hourglass, and a set of hateful, miniature eyes stare back at him from the inside of the glass. The blinking of detached eyes shocks him a bit, but he doesn't lose focus as he eases back down the ladder, treating the placement of his feather-like steps as though he were a bird balancing himself upon a thin telephone wire.

Once he is about three feet from the ground, he takes a leap of faith and creates a cloud of dust as he bounces back onto the floor in one piece.

Ishom places the hourglass on the ground, and Alibabah then pitches himself over Natouja's life key like a tent. Rippling effects of rainbow red, orange and purple stream in a reverse river of peace over Alibabah's spirit as he chants, "Hom bas ho do kra de," draining all forces from her precious life key as he grits his teeth to stomach such a tremendous wattage running through his spirit. This spell will help him inherit a new body, as well as maintain the power to shift the thoughts and decisions of Pharaoh's mind.

Above ground, fox-feathered eyelashes encrust the delicate eyelids of the sleeping Natouja as she rests in her bed. And as she sails through the muddled ripples of REM sleep, a distinctly soft bell dings in the hidden depths of her mind, signifying that the seal on her time capsule has been tampered with. Her eyes flutter like a butterfly emerging from cocoon status, and thirst pockets on her tongue make the muscle in her mouth feel like sandpaper. She howls as the combined sour of heartburn and indigestion pulsate through her throat and blur her vision. While enclosed in her dark bedroom, the queen feels her way around to locate her closet, but sadly trips over her nightstand. Yet she pushes through the irritation of a stubbed toe and an upset tummy to open the closet door and snatch her robe off the hanger, attempting to halfway dress herself.

She leaves the castle and runs toward her pyramid, and beneath her burial site, Alibabah is still at work to penetrate the power of her life key. He looks at it and wonders why it's so damn hard to just fully open the little hourglass. The protective spiritual seal has been removed, but actually opening the damn thing is a headache. This curvaceous spirit key stands up against electric volts and everything. But then he notices a weak point in the center and tells Ishom to take his hands and snap the hourglass in half like a wishbone. The lone set of triple-sized eyes, suspended behind the glass, belong to Natouja's mental eye, projecting forth a look of sheer pity, almost pleading to be left alone. But Ishom does as he's told, and upon cracking the life key open at the midsection, Natouja's whole soul is manifested into plain sight. It looks just like her, but is sheer, yet definitely present as it is bound under a heavy charm. The being's ankles begin to buckle. And just as her set of eyes grew instantaneously and ended up manifesting into a full-size spirit, her soul cells continuously multiply with one another, increasing the size of her spirit in height, width and depth. As a result, she becomes the size of the average human being.

Everything else that was inside the capsule also multiplies upon exposure to the element of oxygen, and although the actual element of oxygen does not exist in this dimension, its effects were still recorded in a layer of time. And what was once the amount of a palm full of sand astronomically doubles over and over again. The mound of sand extends all the way from the bottom of her feet to her breast plate, while she is consumed by all that poured forth from the hourglass, and her spirit is literally buried alive. Then the sand crystallizes as Alibabah gathers what little is left of his electric charge to send a strong current toward the compacted heap of sand.

Back above ground, Natouja queasily walks toward her pyramid and can't help but wonder why the lines between the bricks glow like radiation. This appears to be a definite clue that tonight is just not her night! Natouja, in the flesh, turns around and darts back into her palace, and as she races inside, the tail of her nightgown, as well as a few particles of sand, trail behind her.

There are no lit lanterns in the house. All that is visible are Natouja's bug eyes. She shakes in frosty fear, as the damp effects of night chills cause her gown to stick to her skin like fresh sap. It's as quiet as hell right now, but something still doesn't feel right...the dusty air feels really stale.

Faster and faster, the moon swirls from egg yolk yellow to a bloody meat red. The windy elements roar with thirst pockets, desperate to collect somebody's soul tonight. And as she looks out the window, the raging sands have composed a sketch of a devilish face glaring at her. It just sits there, confidently, eerily smiling at Natouja as it nods its head. By that same token, winds percolate toward the house, and then creep underneath the palace doors. Once inside, the rapid twister clusters together in a funneled fashion, cascading across the tile floors. Natouja's knees knock together as she awaits a fortune untold.

The ferocious winds delectably spot the queen, and her eyes narrow as the tornado churns into a satiny silver. It roars as loudly as a train as it picks up speed, and if one could view it in slow motion, he could see that it is composed of a set of clips. Each frame has a beast imprinted on it. But when the animation flows in a streaming motion, it projects a solid beastly creature on the exterior of the twister.

The being's neck and head look much like the Star Wars creature, Chubaka. Meanwhile, Natouja sweats in sheer misery, contemplating what in the hell this thing could be doing in her house. Yet before she can even manage to mouth the question, the animated tornado cocoons her body whole, ripping around her like a hell-bent merry-go-round. A sorrowful song of murderous shrills escapes the tornado on an intermittent basis. And as it continues to ping-pong off the palace walls for an entire minute, the sound disintegrates into a drifting gust of silence. Natouja's pulse-free body then falls like a bag of sticks to the ground, yet still remains intact.

Then the twister and remaining grains of sand on the floor are sucked back through the dimensions of the corners, as well as the windows, as if no one or no being had ever entered the palace. With a smirk painted above his poked-out jaw line, Aliabah's soul watches the whole episode play out through the sliding glass doors. At first, he can't believe it…the queen's soul is finally in the realm of slumber. His shoulders shimmy in celebration. Yet after 10 minutes, this bittersweet reality registers with his psyche. The body is finally vacant. And as he builds up enough courage to step through the glass, he creeps in close and at first he huddles over his mother's helpless body. For the first time ever he can feel the fragrance of her lost innocence exude from her pores. He bends over and softly kisses her cheek, and then goes in for the kill. Huddling over her body like a cloud of death, he manages to shed a tear. Now bearing the proper authority, which he gained from sucking his mother's life key dry, he is able to penetrate her shell via her palms and mouth, intertwining his spirit with her remaining flesh. This type of contact ignites a bright blue bolt that outlines them both with thousands of watts worth of electricity. And from the spiritual to the physical, Alibabah inherits all of Natouja's power, destiny, and prestige!

Now as for Natouja's soul, its sediment has been retracted back into her tiny life key as retro physics permits. The distant keepers of the realm of rest chose to repair the crushed hourglass and wasted sand to the point of perfection, and she was then shot up into the night sky like a star, stationed gently by the moon.

Ishom then knocks on the door, and Alibabah, who is now in the form of Queen Natouja, chooses to slide it open to get his brother out of the cold. The two just stand there in silence until Alibabah blurts out the secret code they had both agreed upon to signify that the transformation actually went through: *'My Brother's Keeper.'* And Now Ishom is certain that the spiritual exchange was successful and it is truly Alibabah who occupies Natouja's shell. The vibes of love flow freely as the two brothers share a firm embrace filled with the joy of the very thought that they will now be able to deceptively rule a nation as Mother and Child, and no one else will know it but them!

CHAPTER Ten

Hail To The Queen

The next day, the magnetic core of Alibabah's soul continues to breathe life into Natouja's boastful torso. Her likeness extends its arms like a victorious genie as Alibabah uses her shell to bask in his first actual stretch of sunlight, which can be felt in human form. It's almost as if time has slowed down to totally process the new queen's electric presence. Her buzzing aura clusters and compresses all of the microscopic, molecular atoms, which compose the three dimensions of self: mind, body and soul. Now, to the human eye, all one can see is her radiant, royal glow. But the shimmering residue from the old queen's energy mixes with his electric waves, winding around Natouja's revived corpse in a sea of consciousness. These ripples illustrate the power of the human mind.

Further positioning himself down into Natouja's body, Alibabah continually lowers his spirit into her dimensions, sure to replace the queen's soul. He smiles devilishly. In the past, he grinded his teeth down to a stump in agony as he laid in wait for 15 long years, counting down to the moment when he would be allowed to potentially collect a human portal that is strong enough to house such a horrifyingly genius mind as his.

All the tiny bubbles that orchestrate his spirit viciously vacuum themselves toward the queen's core, moving like a symphony of music notes on a fresh sheet of wavy existence. These atoms then fall out of vision as they are engulfed by the darkness of Natouja's navel. She, who is now truly a he, sways in the melody of delight and freedom since he has now been given the sole power to rule in royal form.

Yet his newfound senses still flutter with excitement. The entire world is anew! Craving to experience the fragrance of fresh linens time and again, he hustles back inside as the trail of daylight is dusted off his back as he exits the deck. Now wrapped in the coziness of a partially lit room, it seems that the radiance of life is increasingly surging through his veins as the balls of his feet take in the cool effects of the marble floor.

He showers in the happiness of now having human powers and the ability to swing a fist in anger, or to feel the softness of a loving touch. Yet ragged traces of his mind still can't help but helplessly reminisce upon the times when he used to just watch his twin brother utilize his senses, while he was trapped behind the sliding glass door of the spirit world. Countless times he can recall how Ishom would grin with his arms wide open as he had the ability to know what disintegrating sea lilies felt like as they brushed by his face. He watched him laugh as they tickled the tiny pieces of hair in his nose. Those were the sad days to have to live vicariously through another individual.

But now he is human…oh yeah…now this is his chance to live the good life! He races across the room, and right at the moment when he is at the foot of the bed and prepares to jump in and soak up the freshness of the sheets, Ishom twists the golden bedroom doorknob, holding a scroll in-hand as the papyrus flies through the air. He then hugs his brother, who is still in the form of Natouja, as they fall down on the linens. With rosy cheeks and anticipation, he lets him know that, as planned, Pharaoh approved his early coronation. He lets Alibabah know how many guests to expect…the patterns needed to complement the party plates, as well as the decorative invitations that they still need to choose before sending them out.

Yet Alibabah yawns as he rolls over and gives his brother a dazed look as if he has no idea what's going on. He anxiously hands Alibabah a bag of scrolls to announce the inaugural feast scheduled for next weekend. A wisp of silence is then reinforced as Alibabah callously rolls his eyes, patting his brother on the head, and then pulling the covers up to slurp in just one more ounce of precious sleep.

Ishom can't help but notice that his brother doesn't seem to share his same level of enthusiasm, so he nudges his shoulder to try and get his attention again. But Alibabah simply pulls the covers a little bit closer and balls up to tune out his brother's annoying moans. Yet when he notices that there's no end in sight to silence his noise, he pulls out the weapon of cowardly anger.

Buried in a sea of cottony covers, only his eyes are visible as his pupils thin out like those of an angry rattlesnake. He hisses, "Now look here, little boy, I promised you that I'd get Pharaoh off your back and that you'd be the king, period! But I didn't say exactly when it was gonna happen, now did I? You need to quit being so damn overzealous! Lighten up a bit. We've got all century to throw a ton of balls. What makes tonight so special?"

Alibabah then rubs his shoulder, remarking, "Besides, I don't feel so great. I'm a little achy and oh has this woman's body seen better days…How about you give mama a little backrub, huh?"

Ishom's face reaches a cherry state of red as his eyes blacken with the fall of the night sky. He can't help but gasp as he calls Alibabah out, reminding him that the agreement was that they'd both rule, together. He then threatens him. Balling up his fist, he lets him know that if his senses say he's in pain right now, then he'll gladly introduce him to a heightened experience of human discomfort.

The sheer idea that his little brother would even dare insult him with the spook of a threat enrages Alibabah, fueling the constant flame aglow inside his belly. He picks him up by the neck, wrapping his now polished nails around his throat, whispering, "Listen child, *I* am still the queen of *this* nation, and you'll be beneath me only if I will it so, you son of a…"

"Well then how about Mom, huh? Did she have to go because she gave birth to you? You liar, you need me because the royal power is instilled within both of us!"

Alibabah blinks, wondering if it could really be true that they are both spiritual heirs to the universal powers. He closes his eyes to see through a cement wall as he would usually do when engulfed in the spirit world, but the words of his brother ring true. His vision is blocked, and he grits his teeth with the idea that the little twit must've tricked him!

Ishom smiles, letting him know that in reality, he had tricked himself since he lost an abundance of his power when he stepped into another body.

At this moment, knowing they even came from the same womb sickens them both, and disdain fills the air. The bond of loyalty has definitely been compromised. But in the midst of this emotional furnace, they still realize that they both need one another in this world. Ishom needs Alibabah to bear the image of the queen to the people so all goes well, and he is crowned as king.

In turn, Alibabah needs his brother because he now possesses a stronger connection with the spiritual banks of knowledge. This realm is closely linked to Kullah, which is the central point of the universe. This is the doorway that houses any blessings and holds the manuscript of destiny that forecasts any devastation that can be avoided, and this information is quite handy when ruling a nation. Family is family, but right now, this is purely business as the CEOs of this nation must uncomfortably digest the memo!

CHAPTER Eleven

Dangling Disaster

The scene temporarily closes as the sheer white drapes are drawn, completely casting out the sunlight from the royal retreat. Michael's soul momentarily detaches from his Egyptian past life and he finds himself going up. Elevator tunes play as his soul travels north through the towers of time. He rubs his head, wondering what the hell could be going on right now as he bypasses intersecting strings of light. This type of illumination is representative of one's life track. The strings are comparable to those that decorate a Christmas tree, and each bulb symbolizes a person's major life events in the series of human existence: a first love, the first trauma that weaves the encoding for the wiring of the brain. It also designates who you'll marry, when you're set to have kids, etcetera. Michael is mesmerized as he takes in a dazzling wedding photo that's been impressed against a beaming light bulb. It shimmers like a disco ball, and this is all fresh information as his soul soars upward in a glass elevator. He then reaches a softly illuminated portal where he hears a ding as he stops at the 31st floor. His eyes barely open as he sees a pure white light peeking through the closed doors of the pod-shaped elevator. The double doors then open and mist sprays forth. As he strokes his hair back, he comes even closer to the source of the glow. It's like a center stage spotlight that's being cast completely in his direction, yet all he can think about is how he just wants a warm towel to dry off his bare body. All of a sudden, Dape emerges with a light around her as her hair flows with a bright grin painted on her face as she welcomes him back home. Knowing that the chilly change in temperature took place as he got further north, she removes her shawl and wraps it around him, asking, "So what do you think of this so far?" He stops, sits down and ponders if she is asking him about his recent past life regression, or if she's alluding to the vast concept of space travel overall.

Reading the squiggly lines of curiosity between his eyebrows, she smiles and lets him know that it's okay to be out of words right now. She goes on to tell him how his mind is now processing data at a level of 30 percent, while the average person only uses a little less than 10 percent on a daily basis. So it's normal to be out of words and tired right now.

He giggles a little bit, explaining how the bubbles of space's version of breathing air give off the tingling effects of sparkling water. He's shallowly breathing as he smiles, wondering what's ahead on this journey. He is dampened with perspiration, so Dape leads him to the sauna area to the left to reenergize with a hot cup of chamomile tea. With a towel wrapped around his waist, he sits there…steam rolling off his bare body. The heat breaks up the cool course of his blood flow and he pummels through the process of rationalization to try and understand why he has to go through such extreme life lessons. On top of that, these are distant lives he can barely remember anyway, but the fact that he must relive them is giving him a slight case of anxiety.

His hand trembles as he takes another sip of tea to calm down and stop the jittering of his left eye. But he hears a knock at the door that interrupts his search for internal peace. Dape kindly lets him know that she's in the lounge when he's ready, and he decides that right now is just as good a time as any. He notices that she left him a pair of jeans, a T-shirt, some flip-flops, as well as undergarments on the side bench. As he then exits to the right, passing through the main break room, he finds Dape at an empty table. Her hands are folded on top of a treasure map of some sort, and when he takes a seat, he can see his orange-highlighted course on the roadmap to the sacred city of Kullah, with a small compass kindly marking his current location.

It appears as though he's at the 3/4 mark toward his destiny, but his health is slowly fading. He asks Dape how the virus is still affecting him since he's supposedly in spirit form right now. And she paints a picture for him, showing him the spinning globe of Earth. Its outer lobe is called the ether, and once outside of this realm, there are a series of still shots that make up the future and what will still come to pass in the physical. The progressive concept of front to back still holds true in the outer limits of spirit, yet what is referred to as small pictures are meant to tell the tale of what is to come, and when time tracks bend, they can sometimes get interwoven with the present or the past and so can their effects. This is what happened with the virus when the principle of acceleration got jumbled with the strings of the past.

She also lets him know that this is a difficult concept to grasp at first, and then tells him that the virus is also strong because the universal component of speed got attached to the virus through Satan's multiplied manipulation of the media. Networks have broadcasted that the disease is spreading from country to country, and though these reports did cause the CDC to work triple time to combat global fear, the overwhelming power of fear is crippling society as a whole, and all who have the HIV virus. In the time track of the future, science has come up with a new oral vaccine that does relieve the discomfort of the symptoms for long stretches of time, and in a still shot in his file of the future, he is prescribed the medication. Yet the deterioration of human life in the NOW track, due to the plague, is in a way counteracting the effects of the drug in his system. Almost how you can take two steps forward, yet take one backward and never progress from the midpoint. Therefore, Michael is able to cope with the disease, yet is never able to gain full control over it.

She passes him a vial of the medicine from the future, but warns him that it is only a temporary fix for what he has. As he travels in spirit, he is in a way suspended between the web of time; therefore, he needs to double the effects of his journey to Kullah in order to capture the virus and eliminate is potency. He takes a shot of the lime green elixir, but doesn't feel too different at first. Yet the paleness of death is slowly drained from his pores, and he is able to speak in a clear voice again. Mike asks her how he can complete this mission at double the rate given his current health. Dape then lets him know that learning how to perceptively process the power of **intention** will be his saving grace in this matter. He slightly raises his neck, as his ears perk up, while she places a pen on the table, balancing it on its point.

"How are you doing that, Dape?" he asks. She calmly explains to him how this is simply the ability to hone the power of intention. All things stand and they can also crumble given the intention of the individual. Intention is closely tied to the concept of karma, and it is one's intention that governs the effects of the consequences that will follow the action. That's the concept on the earthly level. But one can crush glass or breathe life back into someone who has already passed away, all by processing and channeling Intention. He asks her how long the pen will stand up like that without support, and she suggests that he intertwine his mind with the pen and imagine that he is one with the utensil. He skeptically closes his eyes and the gravitational waves of his mind connect with the pen as he straightens out his back, mimicking the linear structure of this object. The moment he does this, Dape whispers to him that he needs to absorb the object with the fibers of his mind. His mind is now dark, and all that he sees through his mind's eye is the whiteness of the ink pen.

Dape says, "You are the pen, Michael, now feel the effects of fall across your skin. Imagine all the brown and red leaves blowing across the park sidewalks as you pass by on a cool Saturday. This uses some principles from quantum mechanics, and I know it sounds a little crazy at first, but imagine that you are those leaves, Michael." He seeps into a dream state, softly lowering his eyelids as she continues, "Now allow yourself to run free and disperse with the effects of nature for a moment!"

He feels a small, fiery spark inside the depths of his belly as he tries to apply what Dape calls the power of intention. In his mind, he sees the fallen leaves blow by his feet as he reminisces about the long walks he used to take as a teenage boy. Euphoria builds within his heart pipe, but he and the flowing leaves are not one yet. Biting his bottom lip, just a little bit, he appears to catch the concept as he mentally recreates a breeze. It blows up the side of his neck. The tiny pieces of hair rise on his skin as well, and he unclenches his fists, placing them on the table, and then lets the memory pass from his belly to his upper body. Just like that, the pen falls over and rolls across the porcelain tabletop onto the floor. He opens his eyes in amazement of what he just managed to accomplish, simply by housing the power of intention.

Dape adds, "See Michael…very few people combine what I refer to as aligned faith with the prophecy of intention. This is how you can speed up your journey…by intending to walk through your form of reality. You have to visualize your destination with an extreme amount of intensity. And this is how you bring to pass what you imagine in the course of your reality."

Flattening the creases in the map, Dape calculates Michael's precise location in the field of his destiny and compares it with the hidden pyramid, which marks the entrance point of Kullah. She continues, "Now when you locate this hidden city, you'll have what is called a knowing within yourself to let you know that you have arrived."

Michael smirks a bit, because all he knows right now is how his body has become weary due to the stress of passing through so many portals of existence as the disease continues to eat away at his mind, body and soul. Dape lets him know that the sheer point of peace and purity will swallow his whole existence as he finally figures out how to unlock the spiritual door, which is lodged in a certain point in time, holding the true cure. But it is highly important to first remember that he must intend to drop any clutches and chains of bondage, which weigh down his soul. This limits the mind as well as the ability to pave an unwritten reality. He unknowingly accumulated many demons throughout his past lives. Some came from generational curses, while other spirits entered through spiritual wounds from past pains. And to enter sacred ground, his mind must be washed free of iniquity and freed from its cousin, anguish. The residue of these things delays the promises of a destined prophecy. With those words, Dape crinkles the map back up while handing it to him as she walks him back to the elevator to finish up what he still has left to conquer in the journey of his Egyptian past life. Yet as the double doors close, she quickly hands him a couple vials of the HIV combating elixir, kissing her palm softly, and then placing it on the elevator's glossy exterior. Michael then returns the gesture and is off to pick back up where he left off in Egypt.

Chapter Twelve

The Celebration

A Night To Remember

It's close to midnight, and as dark Nile waters run thin, the moon glows against the watery reflection as the townspeople clamor across the slightly damp, canal floor, waving their silver-wrapped invitations like celebratory bells. The anticipation sizzles through the cool desert air, and the excitement infiltrates the crowd's aura. They all race for a chance to attend what's been said will be the greatest festival that the east has had in nearly 30 years.

Only the finest food is appropriate for Ishom's inaugural feast tonight. Countless barrels of wheat and milk are poured into giant porcelain bowls, as faithful servants whip it into a silky consistency, while uncorking dark wine. This wine is rich! It is so dark that the maid cannot even see her own shadow in its reflection! This bitter type of potency would quench any man's thirst, and possibly make his sweetest drink his last.

The melody composed of horns and harps resonates through the palace halls as electrified chatter festers on the other side of the door. The guests anxiously await the stroke of midnight so they can enter.

The bulging arms of the guardsmen extend in unison to lift a 300-pound piece of lumber from the door handles to permit entry. Not two seconds later, Prince Ishom who is smiling from ear to ear on the third level of the balcony announces to all that it is time to enter. The doors break open with rippling excitement as the guests flood the guarded hallway, constantly crushing petals from dried roses beneath their feet.

The people see who they recognize as Queen Natouja sitting in her ruby-studded throne, and they curtsy in her presence. It's official! Alibabah pulled it off, fooling the crowd by bearing the likeness of Queen Natouja. Ishom then proudly stomps down the main stairwell to greet his faithful followers, kissing all the blushing belly dancers and making strides to join his brother in a sea of excitement. And as he gently caresses the last guest's hand, he takes his rightful seat at the center and enjoys a lettuce roll of crab-stuffed shrimp, covered in melted cheese. He then reaches over to grab Alibabah's jeweled cup, yet it is pulled back, as Alibabah lets him know that only kings can drink from this cup. *A King*, he wonders. But Ishom doesn't just take this jab and swallow it. He bites back this time, kindly advising him that if that's the case, then he hopes that he keeps in mind what is truly underneath his skirt…nothin' but princess panties! Though he is still on rocky terms with Ishom, Alibabah can't help but laugh at that joke.

Meanwhile, the crowd cheers, lifting their diamond-lined glasses toward the suede-draped ceiling, and Alibabah beckons for the maids to refill all cups to the brim. He then flips his hair and asks Ishom to meet him in the center of the room, where a circular pool, 5' wide, is fenced in. Ishom knows this is a cue for the coronation, so he opens the gate and puts one foot in the water to test out the temperature. Then he turns to the servants as they hand him the royal robes, woven of green, yellow and red. Now in the center of the pool, he is elevated by a platform, as he wades in the water, toasting his mother before drinking the darkened wine. And right after Ishom is about to be shrouded with his final garment, a thud resounds throughout the castle, causing the wine in each grail to quiver with the worry of wait.

The people in the crowd duck down until they can figure out if it was lightning that struck the palace or not. Ishom darts to an open window and peaks out as he is merely blinded by the sharp glimmer from the full moon. Disbelief clouds his eyes, yet he wipes them clean to behold the fact that the moon is orange and completely aglow, positioned directly above **Natouja's** great pyramid! Then it swirls from orange to the color yellow before reaching a dreamy shade of gray, and then it turns from grayish blue to gold.

But how could this be? one might ask. Given the timing spell Ishom and Alibabah had channeled upon her soul, the blueprints of history should have been able to suspend the queen from the earth plane for centuries to come!

Perhaps if Alibabah and Ishom had used less time trying to break open Natouja's spirit capsule, and had actually read the inscription at the base of the hourglass, then they would have realized that during a 10-day block in the calendar, they can only suspend her from the third planet, also known as Earth, for one terrestrial night…roughly 24 hours. Timing is everything in the solar system, and the trick is that when a full moon aligns itself with the seventh blessed star of Egypt, it can activate the true owner of the pyramid's soul. This is why Natouja has been given the ability to try and reclaim what she has lost.

Suddenly, Ishom warns the people to look out! The stars illuminate in a zigzag sequence, lighting the skyline from the left to the right, one by one, until the lights flash throughout the gridlines of time. And as they burst and sparks turn to ash and settle on top of the houses in town, the scorching substance continues to burn right through the castle rooftop. Seeping through the cracks, bits of ash then land on a random guest's head, and he repeatedly tries to dust it off in a front-to-back fashion. But the temp on top of his head feels like it's steadily rising, delivering 3rd degree burns to his skin. The man turns to his wife as he wails for her to see what she can do to stop it. With quick-thinking, she wraps his head with her scarf. Yet in a random sequence, the same thing happens to another man in the corner, and then a girl with gentle, dark locks gets a taste of the action as her lovely brown hair becomes toast!

The message doesn't take long to process, and the guests grab their partners and clamor toward the back exit. They make like oxen and trample the delicate rosebuds beneath their feet, permanently coloring the floor into a deep cry of crimson. Yet as they all try to pass through the wooden doorframe at the same time, bodies beat up against one another and splinters get deeply lodged into the flesh of those struggling to run toward life.

Choom—Choom—Choom!

The rest of the shooting stars explode like golden bullets, charring exposed flesh. The vibes inside the palace just went from exuding a bright hue to invoking sheer horror as these desperate people race to flee toward the soothing comfort of sand! In this wave of panic, their skin is being singed, but their bodies have not been fully engulfed by the flames. Yet the crippling effects of fear tend to blind a sane man's vision, making him stop, drop and roll as a survival instinct to seize what is perceived as a fading glimmer of life.

Yet as a number of injured people fall to the floor, many others are able to make it out freely and escape the mysterious ash that scolds the skin like a hot pan of water. Then a wave of wind blows through the double doors, encrusting sand around the brim of the fleeting crowd's eyes. At this very moment in the spirit realm, Natouja's undetected soul suddenly invades the castle.

Not seeing anyone in sight that appears to be plotting enough to fight her two sons and win, her spirit enters a fanged rattlesnake through its beaded tail. Its eyes bloom into full gray, and then the snake's pupils thin out to the width of a dime. The snake charmer puts down his flute to pat his little pet on the head as he prepares to tuck it away and escape as well. But right when he reaches for him, the serpent strangely snaps at his owner, the guy who brings him fat mice every day. Dazed, but not desperate enough to stick around and reach out for another hissing kiss, he wraps his head and ears and follows the rest of the crowd outdoors.

The mouth of the snake curls with pleasure as Natouja uncoils her new, scaly body, while slithering down the straw barrel. Her arrogant aroma places the seven other snakes in sight under a charm, and they can't help but follow her command as her chin is elevated with pride. Since her earthly passing, her connection with the dark arts has been magnified, and she can transform into the likeness of any being, as well as put anyone or anything under a trance to do as she pleases. The pride that comes from having excessive power drip from your fingertips paints a self-assured smirk across her face.

Natouja notices that her twin boys are not present, so she leads the way for the other snakes outside. Once outdoors, Ishom locks vision with Natouja's extremely gray eyes. And even though he can't totally explain what's going on here, he can definitely pick up on the bad vibes that cause his stomach to churn. Meanwhile, Natouja burns with envy. She can see with her spiritual eye that Alibabah's spirit currently occupies her shell like it's nothing, and he looks at her, not knowing that the reptile's scaly skin truly houses Natouja's spirit. He is curious why a snake, a lonesome creature by nature, would be in the midst of all this raucous. They are usually calm animals who like to escape from the heat and lay low in cool, secluded places. Yet Natouja needs to boast herself right now.

She knows that her twin boys still have some power to see into the outer limits of reality and discern a spirit. So she extends the arch of her bendable body, lifting her small head to release a chemical aura that can be detected by one's third eye, displaying her true colors as she projects the radiant image of her soul onto the boy's pupils. Ishom can pick up on her presence like a skunk and alerts his brother that they need to get the hell out of there quick!

But how is this even possible? Well, on the third day of every August, the sun rises slowly as it glows across the Great Lakes. It then trickles down the sides of the pyramids and lands dead smack in the middle of the valleys of the Himalayas. Many tombs are here, and some of the bones of fallen soldiers still remain frozen intact beneath the icy lakes for a purpose. Their skulls wait to recapture spirits like the ones that they have lost. And others remain vacant for reasons unknown.

But they're all the faithful who lurk throughout the trenches of Normandy and Shiloh. They were the last of the fierce to fight and defend their kingdoms. By that same token, Natouja bears a similar vengeful spirit, but one that is perfected through the virtue of patience. Sure, she gave birth to these men, but they launched her spirit toward the stars with the intent to lose her in the translation of time. Therefore, she now has no problem pulling them back into their web of karma. Though a mother's love is strong, Natouja just refuses to remain captive to the gods so someone else can roam the earth in her skin!

Now that her spiritual senses are heightened, she can now see how Ishom and Alibabah's souls are conjoined by a sturdy, mental thread. How funny it is to find out that the mad boy was telling the truth all along when he said that Alibabah's soul was still bound with him on Earth! Oh well, somebody's still gotta die tonight!

Just like the spirits of Normandy and other regions extended, Natouja is a sure fighter, and if she brought them into this world, then she can surely take them out of it!

"Come here!" she hisses. "I refuse to lie in your shallow graves! That moon should've dawned on your heads, not mine!"

She then slithers up the side of the castle with lightning-like precision, leaping off the bricks, aiming to strike Ishom at eye level! He tries to pry his mother's fangs off his face, but they only sink deeper into his flesh.

The former queen then narrows her eyes as she releases venom in the fashion of a heroin needle. In the distance, Ishom cries out to his dear brother for help. As Alibabah pulls a pocketknife out of his brassier, he yanks the snake off his brother and dissects the attacker into two pieces. As puss explodes across the sandy desert floor, the snake's eyes slowly shut to embrace what appears to be an eternal sleep. Soon after Ishom dusts himself off and Alibabah cleans off his blade, the newly-crowned prince wipes the sand from his eyes only to bear witness to the fact that their nightmare has only multiplied itself. The dying rattlesnake only regenerated as its sores healed, and now two snakes sway in a deceptive aura of peace across the desert floor.

Alibabah grabs Ishom by the shoulder, but the little king quickly passes out. He then drapes his brother's arm around his neck and races inside the still smoldering household to a safe place.

In the midst of this utter battle, Ishom wonders if the smoke has made him a bit delusional as the mental image of a purple elixir appears in the back of his mind, and its liquidity resembles the softness of purple silk. With jittery nerves, he murmurs to Alibabah that somethin' purple might calm her down, and Alibabah doesn't quite understand how a simple color might cause a snake to hibernate its fangs, but not knowing what else to do, he tells Ishom to throw his purple sash at the oncoming twin rattlers to blur their vision. Now this was an idea, but it surely wasn't a good one. The snakes simply whip sideways in unison to dodge the diversion and close in on their kill.

Meanwhile, Alibabah and Ishom pick up speed and manage to scurry behind the secure walls of the guestroom, kicking the door closed. He wonders why his own mother would bother to act this way, but the puzzling look on his face blooms into full-blown horror in sight of what lies ahead.

Sure, Alibabah slammed the door shut, but Natouja is working double-time in snake fashion. She feels so betrayed by the boys that she had once loved dearly. So she manages to thin herself out, deflating the girth of her tightly coiled skin to slither beneath the bottom of the guestroom door. As one snake manages to make it through, it shrills about two seconds later in pure pain as Alibabah stomps its guts out to let Natouja know that she is not welcome in here.

Natouja feels a tad bit defeated, yet is still operating off the adrenaline rush of anger. So the other snake gnaws small mouthfuls from the bottom of the wooden door to create a clear gateway and make it through a bit quicker. Just like an ant that makes a new home in the sand, Natouja sees some progress, but it is so minimal that she loses hope. So she expands her mind in a new direction to see how else she can get into the room.

Ishom asks Alibabah to let her in…for god's sake she's still their mother. Maybe a resolution can be reached or something. Yet Alibabah just looks at him crazily. He sits down on the bed, with his hand on his chin, and then grabs a vase with a 9" circumference to illustrate his point. He holds the vase up and asks Ishom if he really thinks that Natouja intended to possess a snake's body with a similar girth to drum up peace talks! With his hand on his hip, he then points at her stolen body, which he still occupies, exclaiming, "She wants this, but she ain't gettin' nothin'! Not tonight, not now, not ever!"

He releases a huge sigh, explaining that if she could have just stepped outside of herself for one moment, then things would've been great! He reminds Ishom of Natouja's god-given strength to channel things that are unseen into the 3-D realm. But she's never used her gift to help anyone besides herself. She's just selfish! Yet the gods never take a gift away, so she is allowed to continually bless only herself.

He then adds that she could've just simply asked the great ones to spare his life as an infant, and then none of this would be happening right now! But she didn't. She secretly thought it would be *so* much easier to just keep one son and eliminate the possibility of a split household. So she pretended to be sad as if she didn't know that she was pregnant with twins. But the truth is that she felt two heartbeats throughout her entire pregnancy, and the gods provided her with spiritual enlightenment to let her know that one son's heartbeat was scheduled to fade soon after birth. She processed the information, yet was secretly happy that she wouldn't be the victim of a split household. But being the drama queen she is, she put on a show and pretended to be sad to see her firstborn die so suddenly. When Natouja chose not to revive Alibabah, the decision was right for the kingdom, but it did not demonstrate the loyalty that a mother should have toward her son! Damn…isn't family supposed to mean something?

Ishom slowly builds consciousness again, and as he builds up enough energy to lean against the windowpane, a white horse's hooves burst through the glass window as the beast screams, "Come here you son of a… You took what's mine, but I'm gonna repay your thievin' ass tonight! Now hand it over!"

But they're not letting go of a good body so easily…oh no! Ishom throws back his shoulders to ward off Natouja's demonic presence, yet the horsepower he's encountered is a bit stronger than what he had forecasted. Ishom's clothing is suddenly snatched up by Natouja's right hoof, and in horse form, she bangs his head against the wall several times until his body begins to shiver.

Ishom then grabs the closest weapon in sight, which happens to be a relatively small statue of the goddess Isis. And with a pointy trinket in-hand, he now has something strong enough to kind of match the impact of a hard, flesh-cutting hoof. To put an end to this madness, he and the horse go tit for tat!

Blood spirals across the walls as if the ghost of a raging Picasso decided to stop by and paint the bedroom. It is frightful as it looks just like the red residue of war. Ishom crouches down and his knees are knobbing like a frightened skeleton, but he must finish this. Right when the horse is about to pummel him, he sets down the pointy tip of the statue and wounds the animal as it falls upon his trap. Meanwhile, Alibabah's nervous system has automatically shut down with overblown shock! Ishom's muffled cries then slowly seep into his brother's earlobes, causing his heart to pump enough blood through his veins and soothe his cold body to unclench his shaking fists. He then flips onto his stomach and crawls toward the closet to grab a sword.

On the other side of the room, Ishom's flesh is getting bruised more and more with each passing moment. Though Ishom hit a main nerve in the horse upon sudden impact, essentially paralyzing the animal, Natouja is still close enough to snap her jaws at his exposed flesh, slowly bringing forth a wound on Ishom's body. This is an attempt to slowly bleed him dry.

Alibabah currently witnesses his brother's attempted murder, and he stumbles as he drags a sword behind him and then pulls his brother away from the scene. Natouja's horsey head wiggles in panic mode as her bright eyes take in the reflective nature of the sword. At first he taunts her, lowering it no more than two feet every time he drops it down to her nose. He has a sinister grin on his face while he grips the handle. Natouja wants to take off, but she's paralyzed on her side and horses don't possess the ability to crawl; therefore, No Grip + Massive Weight = Dead Weight. And with three clean swipes from the razor-sharp blade, her stubborn head comes clear off and stops shaking. Man wins this beastly exorcism, and Natouja's soul is now released, free to hunt for her next vehicle.

Meanwhile, Ishom pulls his knees in tightly and Alibabah uses a sash to wrap around his brother's open sore. But the wound is too big now. Not even a double grip of applied pressure can cease the bleeding. Alibabah looks at Ishom and asks him what he should do. Ishom simply asks his brother to cradle him right now as he strives to mentally relive his lessons of Tai Chi. His instructor once told him that to push beyond pain, one needs to channel the element of mental intention to heal the body. He chants a healing melody in a sad, ghostly pitch in order to activate the pure power of healing. Ishom then closes his eyes and envisions that he is healthy and active again at his martial arts class. He generates healing heat through his body as well, and as a foggy vapor seeps from his pores, the sore begins to mend itself with fastening patches of scabbed skin. As Alibabah's true tears fall onto his brother's flesh, the bitter salt doesn't pain him, but the power of love and compassion cause the scab to sew itself shut even quicker. Ishom then crouches forward, slowly elevating upward into the independent posture of a wide stance.

He has a sparkling vibe of invincibility, encircling him like Halley's Comet, and the spirit of fear instantly flees from his soul. Yet he suddenly remembers that the soul of a tireless predator is dead set on his early extinction, so he comes down to reality really quick to compose a plan of destruction for Natouja.

Yet Alibabah is still flabbergasted from Ishom's expedient recovery. His hands shake with anxiousness as he is eager to know how he could have healed himself so fast. But his tongue refuses to unleash the correct composition of words in order to form a clear question. Full of confidence, Ishom lets him know that he'll explain the power of intention to him a little bit later in the game. But right now, it is imperative for the brothers to conjoin forces and find out how to take down an already ailing queen…quickly! Ishom then grabs Alibabah's flimsy hand and directs him to the hidden lair of mirrors.

CHAPTER Thirteen

The Hidden Portals

The guest door gently cracks open and the boys' shadows prowl against the tall hallway ceilings in a mood of hunt. Ishom then enters the coal-colored den entrance to adjust the squeaky, full-length mirrors, and Alibabah stumbles behind him as the lookout for anything that moves too quickly across the floor. First, Natouja had taken on the form of a snake, and then she inhabited a horse to kill them. An aura of anxiety encompasses the boys as they wonder what she'll pull next!

And just as they make their way down to the lower level of the den to flip the last of the three mirrors over and dust them off, Natouja's thin, ailing soul appears in an air of dominance. She's tired and her soul is losing its coloration in areas like her stomach and torso. One can see through the bottom of her belly to her intestines, and her right arm is barely visible; only translucent specks of her soul are present. She looks like a worn-out Monet, yet arches her back to mimic the impression of superiority. A tear then quivers down the side of her cheek. She is dying because she needs a whole body right now! With her failing health, the minimal effort to take in a healthy breath felt like she had just breathed in a pail of vaporized liquid nitrogen. Without a body, she is getting weaker by the moment.

Ki-cow, ki-cow! the crow cries from above to alert the queen. As it lands, Natouja pats the bird on the head to reward loyalty, and then beckons for her boys to come forth.

They bury their necks in their shoulders, not wanting to be seen by the evil queen. But it's too late for all that. And although Alibabah possesses the captured appearance of Natouja, his mother can still spot the true identity of his soul.

She waves, replying, "Good evening, boys! Are ya hungry?"

At that moment, a jackal creeps from behind her, displaying his 2" teeth. Nature is currently under Natouja's murky charm right now, and the darkness vested inside of the animals causes them to align with the queen's murky spirit and obey her every command. The dark resurrection of her tomb summoned these animalistic warriors to fight for her and give her all they've got until there's nothing left and all energy has been concentrated into fueling her cause.

She sits tall like a proud woman, but if one were to stand still long enough, you could actually hear her bones softly crumble. Her energy level is steadily depleting as she dwindles in the balance beams of reality without a physical shell that can regulate the electric volts of her spirit. As a result, she needs to connect to a sturdy, human portal to ground out the energy frequency that rapidly rushes through her at 100 mph. In the spirit realm, the radiation of the electromagnetic field is heightened, and the protective, human shell is no longer available to regulate fleeting trails of electricity. Another person's mood change, as well as different clips of time, can penetrate the dimensions of the soul, constantly interrupting a state of peace. To put it blank, Natouja is not fully human yet, and that'll only take place once her body has been restored and rightfully returned to her. So she just sits there, watching her darling little boys stand in shock like a pair of frozen deer in headlights.

The sound of decay comes forth again. Her frame weakens like a rotting stack of wood with every passing moment. Her soul desperately needs to be replenished at once. So the jackal's finely tuned ears hear the decomposing cry of her failing frame, and he then leaps to her aid, capturing the crow in midair, while quietly dismembering it. Natouja's eyes flutter with the intensity of excitement as she gets ready for her liquefied feast. The animal stands up on his hind legs to let her know that it is time to drink, and she meets her furry friend at eye-level to extend her tongue and lap up the bloody bird's sacrifice.

As a result of her feasting, the right side of her face begins to gently stitch itself, miraculously forming new flesh that wasn't there before. Licking her lips, she deems the drink to be delicious. Blood continues to splash across her cheeks, and as she wipes her mouth clean, the boys' feet begin to make tracks toward her vase of jasmines. Yet the jackal angrily stomps toward them to bring their mission to a halt.

Alibabah and Ishom notice that they're being followed, and before their knees buckle, they manage to scram in opposite directions. Natouja's frosty eyes turn to a high tint of silver with the intent to react two steps ahead of their plan.

With the strength of the crow, her spirit flies forth and enters the jackal's body, engulfing the creature in a blue flame that doesn't damage its body. Yet her energy gives him boundless strength. The animal's eyes melt into the smooth color of gray, and the queen's soul inhabits her newest carriage!

Dashing, sprinting, and knocking everything over in the path that leads toward the jasmines, the boys leap like dazed frogs for their very lives, as she snarls, "Don't you dare touch my jasmine tree!"

But Alibabah grabs it off the mini tabletop and smashes the vase against the wall anyway, and as he rolls around in the fallen petals, he hopes that they could provide some sort of ancient spell of protection since Natouja was always known throughout the land for casting devilish spells. But sadly neither white, nor black magic has been instilled into the composition of these buds. They are just that…buds. Natouja always boasted their greatness and guarded them as if they were magical, but there's really nothing truly special about them.

Meanwhile, Ishom is moving about the outskirts of the room, laying a whole set of tea candles on the floor in a circular fashion to get ready for their own version of a black magic boogey. Natouja gains speed and rapidly approaches her mischievous cubs to implement tough love and take a nice chunk out of Alibabah's deceitful soul!

Just a side note…when Mommy tells you not to touch that shrub, no matter how abstract the concept is, you must obey her wishes in order to avoid getting that tail popped! It's just that simple. Another thing, when Mama is trying to sleep, it's just not cool to wander into her cave and help yourself to her life key. These are just basic courtesies.

Yet her boys are beyond the rearing stage when they can still be taught, so screw the concept of reasoning with them! So as her fangs pierce Alibabah's throat slowly, careful not to mar her own body, Alibabah's eyes become as white as a ghost. Sure…he struggles to break free, but his demise is purely inevitable.

Natouja's eyes tear up just a bit. Somehow he managed to tap into a part of his mother's heart that hasn't been charred by repetitive disappointment and regret. Feeling a shred of maternal sympathy, she closes her eyes, snapping his neck quickly, and then digests his strength into her expanding belly. How ironic! In a way Alibabah returned to the womb…the same place that once guarded him and Ishom as infants.

But she's not finished just yet. Once Alibabah's spirit is free, it fades into the outer realm of existence since he was unable to quickly attach to Ishom's energy field once more. The jackal pinches his eyes shut upon the moment that Natouja exits its body, and just like the vapor of an exhale on a frosty winter's night, she soars free. Her vaporized soul violently flutters through the animal's retracting lungs, and then flows from the jackal's mouth cavity right before she slides back into her body! She first licks her face clean again before reentering her shell. She then gets situated. There, there, that's it! She gets cozy in old skin again as if she were trying on a stylish dress about two sizes too small. Simultaneously, the waves of consciousness cocoon around her revived corpse as she becomes completely whole again! Her mission is complete, and the true queen rises once again to reclaim her kingdom.

She slaps her voluptuous backside, gripping her scepter tightly, as she proudly approaches the centered, full-length mirror. As she wipes the foggy dust off its reflection, and adjusts her platinum crown so the centered ruby reacts proudly amongst the descending diamonds, her smile is a bit crooked, much like the body of a tiny garden snake. She thinks she's made it out just fine and all will be hers again, yet little does she know that she has stepped into the seventh circle of the portal. While she was busy warding off Alibabah, Ishom took an inch-long piece of chalk and drew the witch's sphere on the floor. This powerful symbol is comprised of many circles within a circle, much like a target, and whosoever steps into the center of it will supernaturally have all of his chakras opened and aligned, and the subject's spirit will be under the control of the master who drew it.

Natouja rubs the side of her arm as her senses become aware that something is just not right in the air. The atmosphere is chilly, causing her to quiver, but she can't exactly pinpoint the direction of the oncoming draft in this dark room. Yet a circle of lit candles surrounds her and the wind picks up speed, whipping her hair around and around, yet not extinguishing any of the tea candles.

Then, from the back of the room, Ishom flips the last mirror around and Natouja yells like a coyote that was just put out of its misery. Due to the curse of the witch's sphere, she is now coated in a supernatural blue flame and is paralyzed. Meanwhile, her image is instantly broadcasted across the reflection of all three mirrors, yet in each one, she is depicted in a different time warp.

The first one reflects the occasion of her first birthday party. Then the second one tells the time of when she knocked out her head kung fu instructor and rattled the gym floor. The final mirror displays the image of her holding her darling jasmines all aglow. An aura of glitter sparkles around this particular mirror, and its reflective tint is a bit brighter than the others. It's almost as if a soft, summer day gently sways the purple petals in a heavenly tune.

As Natouja witnesses herself in the mirrors, her heart chains become heavy as she recalls the depth that follows the experience of an emotion. The sheer horror of losing any type of emotional control and having her true self revealed turns Natouja's stomach into a smoldering furnace, over-baking her insides and blackening her soul. Ishom just smiles at the thought that the spell is working against the queen. If you can't conquer someone in the physical realm, then you've gotta start chewin' away at the spiritual self first. And although he's happy that he's fighting the queen in another way, the realization dawns on Ishom that he's without the companionship of his twin brother for the very first time in his life. And just as the thought seeps into his mind to take a dip in the shallow pool of self-pity, he decides to face his main problem at-hand right now and musters up the courage to swoosh down the lump of fear lodged deep inside his throat to take down his enemy.

CHAPTER Fourteen

The Deeper Picture

The two stand there in front of the mirror as Natouja is paralyzed by the pain, making her unable to even move her bottom jaw. The constant flames feel like one-thousand needles that take turns jabbing her supple skin. She looks like a frightened, melting doll that doesn't know what's going to happen next. She extends her flaming palm toward Ishom, mouthing for him to please help her and give her a second chance. She knows that he once truly felt something for her as her son. And although Ishom is controlling this charm and has the power to burn her to a cookie crisp right now, he chooses not to. While chanting, creating a type of time warp in the middle of existence, he takes a giant rubber band and pulls the edges with intensity. It's now stretched so thin that it's almost translucent. The circle's donut hole is now big enough to fit his head through. Natouja's eyes get really big. This looks like it could be creepy, and the fact that she's not in control of evil that is being cast forth makes her legs feel like unfinished Jello. With the elastic circle now securely around his neck, he continues to stretch it out and takes a water bottle out of his bag and soaks the floor beneath him. As he steps into the puddle, Natouja's eyebrows heighten about half an inch. She's super scared now because she recognizes the spell that he's about to cast.

It's closely linked to Satanism, but its powers are much more refined, fueled by the channeling of the familiar spirits, which constantly run across the fields of Earth.

A spell becomes more potent as its force is combined with the power of a human soul. This is also the case when a casting is coupled with the strength of a familiar spirit, which carries the residue of multiple people that it has been attached to throughout the eons. In these cases, a spell gains twice the power because it has been lent a grounding post…someone or something, which is composed of enough physical matter to ground out conflicting electricity. This clears the energy waves and allows one to invoke an earthly spell in its purest, most fragrant form.

Yet at this moment, all three mirrors go blank as Ishom throws a dime onto the wet floor. Latent, electric volts have been generated with the power of his channeling words, sending watts of energy across the concrete floor to travel up the silver mirror stands. All molecules reach their highest potential and the surface of the mirrors melt into silver putty. And out from this putty steps the sleeping soul of Natouja's father. While he rests in bed, like anyone, his spirit is able to travel through the hidden, earthly dimensions, although it is partially bound to the earth zone. At the same time, his physical body is still at rest in his room. In order to teach the queen the true lesson she needs to learn, Ishom has chosen to invoke the wisdom of his grandfather. The old man's spirit drifts toward the center of the room, passing through the table as if it were sheer water. All of a sudden, Natouja gets lost in a crosshair in her mind; the simple sight of her father makes her reminisce upon the days when all she ever wanted was his attention and approval, yet it was withheld like a pearl snapped behind a clam shell.

Trigger shots of anger plummet through her mind as she rattles off every single cuss word of her time. The waves of pent-up resentment give her some power to combat Ishom's charm. Sweat is flying off her arms as she incorporates the use of dirty sign language in her rant, and this is stuff she once picked up as a kid. At this moment, Ishom uses the power of the charm to prompt his grandfather's spiritual vocal chords and recite an ancient chant. His soft tone drifts into a beautiful melody that equalizes all of Natouja's vulgar rage at a sudden point of silence.

Simultaneously, Natouja's hidden cry for help reaches a new level as does her rising body temperature. But the blue flames do not char her shell. The power of love seeps through her father's wording. Not all the lyrics can be understood, but the tone connects with his daughter's heart to move closer toward a peaceful solution. Bearing a genetic link to the subject at-hand, Grandfather channels the air in the room and links everyone together in preparation to view and understand the chapters of time. Combined with Natouja's heightened electrical state, the power is then broadcasted through the old man's heart.

Feeling the gust of an intuitive nudge, he believes that the spirit realm is now raw enough for entry, so Ishom continues his spell to lift the energy levels in the room by racing around the atrium with flaming intensity. At the same time, he grabs the loose edges of the rubber band around his neck and pulls the material outward and then a bit north.

By pulling it in an upward fashion, generating a circle of electric heat, he is allowed to warp time and enter the layers of the past. Ishom then picks up a small candle from the floor and cups the flame with his hand and proceeds to race around the room repeatedly to focus and keep the energy levels high.

The putty surface of the mirrors then crystallizes again. The glass is foggy, but the condensation slowly drips off the center mirror to give way to the image of Natouja in her teenage years. The reflection shows her shoulders back and her chin up high as she exudes a vibration of true self-esteem. She appears to be pleasant in this episode of her life, but then the image becomes muddled as her other self comes into focus. In this snapshot, she is cloaked in a black shawl, and her chin is stationed downward firmly within her neck. Her eyes are of pure chill like the fresh frost of a new snow. Her murky image gives off the vibe of a wolf that has just spotted its lunch. Now this is the inversion of self-esteem…low self-esteem.

Although she is draped in a pure jaguar shawl and is wearing a jeweled crown, which is slightly tilted on her head, the inferiority complex of low self-esteem makes it so the richness displayed on the exterior can never match how she truly feels. In this case, the sufferer must knock down anyone who threatens her illusive sense of self-worth by throwing pebbles at her faulty, protective shield she has built up. This way, no one gets close enough to witness the true problems brewing within. Anyone or anything that could overshadow this clay mask of self-confidence must be disposed of, or made to feel worthless within the predator's presence in order to muffle a contending air of superiority.

To try and heal Natouja's everlasting pain, Grandfather extends one foot forth, poking out his chest to let the reflective light from the mirror shine directly into his heart chakra. The brilliance of the light creates a type of silver screen upon grandfather's torso to broadcast a fortune that has yet to be told. Then an image comes into clear focus. On the screen, a circular, silver section swirls much like a whirlpool, and then as it transforms, the Pepsi symbol is brought into crisp clarity.

Grandfather sings in a note that extends beyond an earthly frequency, which causes the light to shine brighter from his chest, and Natouja, Ishom and Grandpa are all engulfed in the radiance of the sandy, off-white light. Yet the Pepsi symbol flickers in a way. At first the image of the symbol is displayed, and then the scene changes, broadcasting a picture of a vase of jasmine shrubs. These images flicker back and forth almost as if one were flipping through an animated book that gives off the illusion of motion. First the Pepsi symbol is displayed, and then the flowers are shown intact as the slides repeatedly alternate.

Ishom's mind is cluttered in a wavelength of confusion, but he allows himself to be consumed by the imagery to find out how to stop Natouja's reign of terror. As the star-studded tunnel of the universe engulfs them, the session feels like light travel right now. All of them have left the wave of consciousness and taken on universal sight as the stars brush over their blushing cheeks. This is simply a part of the process to unlock the truth from Time's file cabinets. As the film begins to roll and is displayed on Grandfather's chest, Ishom watches the movie starring his mother, Natouja. She's just as radiant as can be looking so peaceful and aglow with the unexpected bounty of a new day. Yet at the same time, a rooted sense of sadness plagues her young soul.

As the film plays out, Natouja is but a girl springing across the meadows of her neighbor's lawn, while she giggles as if she just swallowed a huge gulp of a fizz drink that went down the wrong tube. Baby flowers stud her french roll as her spiraled curls sway in the desert breeze. Tonight is the night that she has counted down to since the first quarter of the year…it's a special night when her best friend is scheduled to have a coming of age festival for all of her closest pals.

Natouja's aura is as fragrant as a honeysuckle as she leaps onto her friend's gold-trimmed doorstep and pounds a familiar knock. Meanwhile, the energy is reciprocated from the other side as her friend opens the door with a big smile. But there's a problem here. Natouja brought wilted jasmines to this party, and these blossoms are completely unacceptable for a celebration of this caliber. Though this mistake may be considered minor in the modern-day world, it was catastrophic in the golden times!

As she passes through the hallway, people narrow their eyes to assess the gift that she has brought, and Natouja can feel the awkwardness rise in the stale air. Yet she pretends to laugh it off. She's the girl that's always lightening up the mood at the party. Though the gift is cheap, her friend maintains politeness and leads her to the gift table anyway. Notice that Natouja's friend was polite, not necessarily what you'd call nice. Nice is something that derives from a genuine emotion. Yet when someone does something that is polite, it is usually to protect one's own image and avoid sanctions from society that punish impolite behavior.

Right now, people are baffled by Natouja's gift. She is supposed to be a princess, yet she didn't even bother to bring a proper gift to this party! Natouja's guardsmen are not scheduled to come back for her until a little after midnight, so she's stuck in an uncomfortable situation with nowhere to go. Everyone else flashes the jewels and unlimited grain they brought to the party, and sheer embarrassment stabs Natouja in her pre-teen heart as the famed prince walks by. She has heard about him for years and wanted to meet this young man since she was 10-years-old. But with broadened shoulders, he walks right by her as if she were a ghost who didn't even exist. He stops at the gift table in an air of arrogance and with a smirk; he gently rubs her wilted jasmine petals and walks away so he is by no means associated with a stingy royal.

Natouja catches a condescending vibe and wishes she could explain the whole story behind her gift without sounding sheepish. Last season, the girl who is throwing the party came to her house and delighted in her bountiful fields of jasmine and couldn't believe how extraordinary they were. She told Natouja that she had come up with a way to germinate a single branch and dissect it into small colonies. And with the help of science, she would be able to multiply one branch into ten and so forth. This way, all her friends and family would be able to enjoy their jaded glory as well. Making a mental note of her friend's request, Natouja brought a few of them for her, enclosed in a rare Chinese vase. The vase alone is worth $300 in modern times, but Natouja was not trying to impress anyone with a gift of monetary value. Her gift came from the heart, and she thought it would be unique with the ability to bless her friend's land with a new type of beauty. This way she could cultivate the jasmine vines time and again. Sure…they were a bit wilted due to the long voyage to a foreign land, but they were still perfectly fit for germination! And this incident stings a little deeper than your average faux pas because when Natouja tried to do something thoughtful, she was made out to look like a fool!

As Natouja's shoulders sink to a new low, her friend comes by and taps her arm with a deceitful grin. See, to women, Natouja has it all: long, flowing hair, a body men salivate after, and the intellect of a genius. There is no way the average woman can compete with her. So to even out the score, her friend sabotaged her by hinting to bring a gift that she knew would make her appear underprivileged and silly. As a result, the famed prince would look down on this beautiful girl and not pursue her as a mate of interest. Though this was cruel, it was still an effective plan. The girl giggles as she passes Natouja and heads toward the prince, leaning on his arm as they share a fruit basket the rest of the night. Painful past insults and betrayals, just like this one, pummel on top of each other and crack a new nerve within Natouja's tender heart. She never had a mother…she died in labor, and her father always wished within his heart of hearts that Natouja had been born a boy; therefore, most of his attention went to Natouja's male cousins and Ishom. She had a very limited amount of support at home, so she leaned on her friends, and girl after girl, who secretly viewed her as a humongous threat, rejected her. Over and over, the jealous ones set her up in one way or another, so the little princess became lost and didn't know who she could trust.

Over time, the hole in her heart grew bigger and bigger. And what started out as a piercing the size of a watermelon seed went uncured, and no one ever substituted the pain with love and compassion. So the seed dug itself even deeper, until one day it finally struck a nerve, an already exposed, throbbing nerve! Just think of going to the dentist's office to get a root canal without any pain killer…yeah…it was just that bad!

Years later the hole still ached, so the heart had to find a way to fill the cavity. And with no support from home, and the repetitive teasing from her wealthy peers about her mishap at the party, Natouja still housed an enormous root of anger within her soul. But as a young girl, she still wanted to fit in with the privileged crowd. She asked some new friends to help her dye her hair to a radiant color in an attempt to reinvent her image…but the boys still didn't pay her much attention. Once one has been branded as a social outcast, the stench travels and anyone who is tied to this individual immediately takes on that title as well. The chatter about Natouja being cheap led to other lies that damaged society's perception of her. These lies had spun from the continual web of gossip. And if a lie is repeated over and over again, it seeps into the subconscious mind, and the person who is being gossiped about is automatically viewed in dim light. After a while, Natouja just wasn't cool on any level.

Not much later, this boy who carried around a mini xylophone, and was known for composing funny lyrics, started to sing songs at the lunch table, and the verses joked about how she was trying too hard to fit in! His words stung horribly as well. He had a special connection with Natouja because this was the first boy she had ever kissed while playing spin-the-bottle as a kid. So her self-esteem dipped down yet another level. Slowly, throughout the entire year, almost all the kids gently cut ties with her to avoid punishment by association as she radiated the stench of insecurity like a sewage plant.

And the extra helping of betrayal from her so-called friends made her feel extremely low on the totem pole. To cover up the holes in her soul, Natouja turned away from all that was positive to embrace a call from the dark side. Even though evil is not an extremely comfortable demeanor, it's far easier to maintain than love because she had already let the spirit of hate check-in and mesh with her soul. She had hate for her father's negligence…then hate for her peers. And within the dark corners of her lonely self, the lower entities became familiar to her.

She was angry; they were angry. It was a matrimony conceived in perfect hell because evil can never tarnish evil. It only multiplies in strength.

Though this hateful substitute partially occupied the hole in her heart, strands of humanity still clung to the corners of it, and oh how they burned! For light and dark can never coexist. So she had to choose which one she would embrace, and then leave the other behind.

Natouja had run into her father's study one day, while he was playing a game of chess with his nephews, and she sought him out for a moment of counsel. He barely lifted his head to acknowledge her presence as he chomped on some rice cakes. Yet Natouja let him know that the problem was serious this time…seriously serious! To appease her anguish, he asked a dear maiden to take her away and engage her in some type of girl talk to soothe her soul, but this wasn't possible as Natouja stomped her foot and demanded his immediate attention. So he picked up his pencil and activity sheet to schedule her in for a one-on-one in a couple of days. She furiously bit her lip and couldn't believe his nonchalant attitude in her obvious state of distress. She was damn near frantic, and he didn't even bother to ask her what the matter was. On top of that, he tried to shoo her away to a new-hire maid who didn't even have an idea of her favorite color!

Yet later on that week, her father met with her as promised and plopped a timed schedule in her hand of all that was to be reviewed during her session as if it were just another chore. The tasks on the agenda were intended to sculpt her into a fit ruler, and these lessons delved heavily into ideas of intolerance and revenge. Great Pharaoh believed that no man was to be trusted and the only comfort on Earth was the fear of the throne. It is challenged by few and respected by all.

He sought out to breed a warrior in Natouja and masked her breasts underneath a fighter's plate as she learned to fear no man through the ability to truly love death. Not only did he strengthen her biceps through repeated Kung Fu lessons and homemade, steel exercising equipment, but he taught her how to break bread with her faithful servants, overhear of their secret plans to escape to their home countries, and then punish them slowly in front of one another with the grit of the blade. She learned that true torture is mostly a mental process and people are controlled through subliminal words and visual expressions. With so much rage, her mind went off the Richter scale, and if a maiden's eye were to even slightly glare at her, then she would escort them to the fields and tell them it was time to gather the fresh linens from the line. Once outside and shaded by wheat fields, she would beat them…some of them to the slow point of death until they begged for her mercy. And after some had expired, she would wrap them up in the sheets and send them sailing away with the sea.

Then, out of boredom, Natouja sought to cross the gender lines and dominate the men as well. So she took up the skill of martial artistry, by which she measured her own strength. And believe it or not, most of her victims were her own guards, the ones who had sworn to protect her very life. This way, Natouja knew they were vulnerable to her because they had been classically conditioned to never lift a finger to royalty under any circumstance.

She attacked them quickly, and would kick, and scream, and claw, or bite at them until her opponents had the utter strength of a crumbling leaf. And as they would sway, their eyes rolled back in their heads, with foaming mouths and all, mumbling for a chance at life. But she paid their requests no mind, and with the quick crack of the spine, their services were terminated.

According to her rationale, their corpses served as graduation cords, which proclaimed that she was superior and worthy of the crown! But behind this cold front, she did find time to nurture a personal project or two, and her greatest release of all was her dear garden, where she nurtured her young jasmines because in her fragile mind these flowers were indestructible.

The jasmines weren't a hit at her friend's party, but Natouja kept nursing them anyway because their scent reminded her heart to always be on guard and expose a kind heart to no man. In her mind, the second you do, people will surely toy with you.

The flowers also symbolized purity because they had never been penetrated by the corrupt scruples of the world. Natouja picked a few of these flowers and kept a vase full of them inside. Over time, the jasmines grew to be the length of one full branch, and then they split into two, and later three. Then on a soft, breezy day when she was speaking with her father, she noticed a passerby wandering about the roots of her magnificent jasmines in the garden, and she drew a thorny rod as she chased this thieving intruder away from her babies.

Even though the ripe jasmine gems had been slightly tainted by human touch, she thought they were still salvageable. So with a sense of emergency, the queen picked the rest of them and rushed her babies inside to be replenished by an entire grail of holy water. But since these broken buds were no longer attached to the mother branch, Natouja feared that they would surely die. The dread that she could touch something and it didn't flourish horrified her, so she drew more water from the belly of her pyramid and shot countless prayers up to the heavens to sustain them in spiritually treated water.

And in the end, she was shown favor by the gods because no matter how minor the request, Natouja still had royal favor. And as royalty, not even the silliest desire goes unheard, especially if the individual's sanity heavily depends upon the result.

So they revived her dying flowers, and Natouja kept them inside the house for protection and later found a way to freeze-dry them. At this point, her mind simply couldn't process the fact that even if they did expire, more would surely bloom next spring. Pharaoh noticed her preoccupation with her flowers and suggested that she fill her time with more useful challenges, so he requested a grandson of her, and she happily complied! Just think about it: A boy is much easier to groom than a flower.

Flesh is trainable, and it quickly obeys one's command. On the other hand, a flower is subject to fluctuating winds, thermal conditions, and pouring rainstorms. Also, if a boy were to fail, you could kill him. But if she were to plant a bad seed of a jasmine, then it is free to eternally repopulate the earth at its own discretion. And in her mind, she just doesn't like the idea of failure.

The film stops rolling, and Ishom makes eye contact with his grandfather to confirm that these events are true, and he nods, confirming that indeed they are.

Grandfather clears the screen, wiping his hand from his chest to his stomach, and then says, "Now you know Ishom, it's much easier to give your crown away to those who don't deserve it. The power of the universe trickles from your fingertips, but you brush it off onto others hoping to avoid the conflict of a destiny unrevealed!

"Yes, fear of rejection did destroy Natouja's heart, but the fear of becoming king in your own right held you back from properly owning the throne. You had the heart of a lion, but the lion never progressed from being a small kitty cat crying for his mother's milk."

As he puts his arm around his grandson, he continues, "Now Natouja and Alibabah were given a tough vine in their family, one that was supposed to crush the wickedness that brewed within the family unit. But unfortunately, your ends snapped under pressure.

"You, Ishom, you were the strong one! You were supposed to be the leader of your pack! You were the holy water meant to quench the thirst of the sour Egyptian desert. It was no accident that you had survived during birth, but not your brother, Alibabah. The gods knew that he was hungry for the power of the throne, and he would have made all people suffer just to appease his own earthly pleasures.

"But you were the honorable one, Ishom. You could have returned his soul to the spiritual realm of Kullah from the get-go! But no, quick to question your own strength, you felt the need for companionship in a new, cruel world. So you allowed his spirit to latch onto your aura and feast off your crimson intuition until he was strong enough to capture a free, human body. But when one didn't come along soon enough, he manipulated you into carrying out his plan!"

Yet Ishom explains that Alibabah set the whole thing up to capture Natouja's life key, and that he was only there to help his brother out. But his grandfather's spirit asks him to examine himself for a moment, and as Ishom lifts his hand and takes in all the detailed swoops on his palm and the width of his fingernails, he can't help but see that his hand is completely maroon. He thought that his red spiritual power, mixed with Alibabah's purple force composed a maroon spiritual potency that could accomplish miracles. But this is not the case.

Ishom actually holds the crimson and the purple power. There was no need to remain intertwined with Alibabah's spirit on the earth plane. The force lied solely within him the entire time! Alibabah only clung to his coattail to drain the remainder of his energy field because he knew that he wasn't strong enough to make it on his own without a live, human channel. He gained access to Natouja's spirit key by manipulating Ishom's aura to detect its location with the third, spiritual eye.

But Ishom's grandfather also admits to partial blame for the current state of the family. Though his body is still in slumber on Earth, his spirit roams free and can now see the proper way he should have groomed his child, and he realizes that he failed by breeding a warrior in Natouja. This is the moment when Grandfather waves his hand across his chest again and reveals the true remedy for any type of pain to Ishom: the circular Pepsi symbol. This symbol is representative of self worth.

Sure, back in ancient Egypt, Pepsi hadn't even been created yet, but the image has been eternally bound in the book of time like anything that is entangled in the wavelengths of the past, present or future, floating throughout the ether. In regards to Natouja's pain, the Pepsi symbol is helpful to demonstrate the explanation of true self-worth.

Grandfather tells Ishom that the red part of the symbol represents arrogance, and the blue part is the opposite: low self-esteem. It is not good to be in the red, nor in the blue. In the blue, you can get lost in a sea of self-pity and never be able to manifest your true worth. On the other hand, it is positive to aim for the wavy white line, which serves as the middle ground. This way a person can respect the truest form of self, as well as others and not only give love, but also receive a boundless amount of it in conjunction with the idea of respect. Grandfather goes on to tell him that part of the purpose on Earth is to reach the highest potential of love, because love conquers all, and if you reach the maximum human capacity, which is roughly 98%, then a man will never feel unworthy or alone. It sits on the opposite end from the curse of hatred. Love binds its opposite and heals all wounds, and Great Pharaoh insists that if he had taught Natouja this principle versus the lessons of bone-breaking, then the family unit would have possibly turned out for the better.

Ishom loosens his lock-vision with his grandfather's heart as the picture fades out of focus and his mind leaves the warmth of the universe and returns to the room as it slightly brightens up. Natouja's knees pop like twigs as she leans over a chair and her energy level reaches damn near zero. She then decays to the ground, crawling toward the corner, weeping uncontrollably and exposing all of her weaknesses.

As the last hook of her soul disconnects from Ishom's aura, she turns as black as coal, and the curse of hatred consumes her body whole, fully setting her soul ablaze. All three mirrors bearing Natouja's fiery reflection burst as she continually disintegrates into a small mound of ashes.

Ishom walks over to his cremated mother and as he kneels down, he cries, running his fingers through the blackened sand that used to be her body. His grandpa insists that she never meant to burn him with her words, but when people are undergoing spiritual tribulation, they are also susceptible to manipulation by lower entities who mean to detour people from nurturing the divine seeds that they've been given.

Ishom cries when faced with the physical evidence of his mother's untimely death, but still manages to keep an ear open to the words of his grandpa. He warns Ishom how the dark forces from within tried to get him as well, and they succeeded! They first attacked him through his mother's bitter tongue, and as he absorbed her distorted view of himself, he then fell fool to the trap of hell's noise, obeying the command to silence his true potential. Though Ishom sobs, his spiritual self finally gets it! You must combine **intention** with a healthy, true view of one's self, i.e., **self-worth**.

His grandfather's spirit evaporates into thin air right when he reaches out to hug him. Ishom screams for him to come back…he still has things he wants to learn from him while in spirit form, but this session is finished. As Ishom grabs at the thin air, trying to grasp his presence once more, his efforts are worthless, because grandpa's spirit has returned to the physical realm to compress back into the form of Mind, Body and Soul.

Ishom picks up a jagged piece of mirror and looks at his reflection, taking in his eyes, nose and all that his true self has to offer. He still cannot fathom that it has been this simple the entire time…it's all how you view yourself and once you see yourself as worthy of a new existence, then whatever you intend to do can be done. Hatred kills and love heals.

Truth be told, on top of Kung Fu lessons, Ishom's grandfather had Natouja undergo mirroring sessions as well. This was an attempt to drain her pain from rejection and balance mind + body + soul to achieve inner peace. He had her stand at the center point of the three mirrors to balance her energy waves for hours. He held a whip that stood for reinforcement, and he rarely had to implement its usage, but the fault in the process that he had overlooked was that all three of her reflections faced west, and this oversight, while practicing white magic, generated an imbalance within her three selves. This way, all the energy currents were set in motion to flow to the left and there wasn't an image to strike to the right and serve as a net and catch her energy and bring it back to the center.

That is the moment when her father should have become hands-on, stepped in front of the very first mirror and posed to the right. This way he would have served as a net to keep the energy circulating, and respect would have naturally bloomed in their relationship after the trust factor kicked in. Just like the concept behind a teeter-totter, a person will naturally go overboard, whether mentally or physically, if no one is there to throw the energy levels back in balance, and that is part of the reason why Natouja continued on a downward spiral, first from a mental aspect, and then those results became prevalent in the physical as she became known as the bone breaker.

CHAPTER Fifteen

A New Circumstance

After Ishom extensively examines himself in the jagged piece of mirror, the image of Dape comes into full clarity as it is enclosed within the dimensions of the reflective piece. In the distance, she looks overjoyed at the fact that he now comprehends a major part of his spiritual lesson to unlock the hidden chamber for the HIV cure. She waves at him from another dimension, beckoning him to step through to the other side and pay her a visit. Now equipped with the power of intention and true self-worth, he sweeps the rest of the broken fragments of the mirror into a pile in the middle of the floor. You can hear the crushing glass as he steps on top of this jagged, little mound. He intends to go see Dape in the outer limits and right when his heart and head jive on a mental frequency of unity, the grinding mirror liquefies beneath his feet and the spirit of Michael is sucked downward toward the chamber of knowledge. Again, suspended in universal time, he slowly travels through the elevator, and then hears the bell go *ding* as he steps onto the 22nd floor. There Dape is, laughing, dancing and all smiles because her guy got the major part of the lesson.

He instantly mirrors her enthusiastic mood and playing it safe, he automatically assumes that the toughest part is over and he can advance to the next level. Invoking the use of psychology, he tries to avoid another space travel episode by telling Dape that he forgives her and won't even ask for anything for all the time he had to spend trying to put together all the pieces of this mind-boggling puzzle.

Sweat dripping from his temples, he desperately awaits her reply, and Dape gives him a mischievous grin because the game is just now getting good!

She leaps into motion, exclaiming, "Ooh, round three, here we go! You learned a little bit in that second life, but your mind still needs to be purified a little bit more to enter the holy place of Kullah. But when this whole thing is over, you're gonna be awesome, I mean so freakin' amazing, Michael!"

Another idea pops into her mind, and as she reaches underneath the table, she pulls out another bottle of potion to start the next journey.

But Michael is simply frustrated, and he lets her know that he's so sick of being flung around from one time warp to another, searching for this cure for AIDS, and he hasn't turned up with anything yet! He explains that something just doesn't feel good about this whole thing.

Michael then flings off his jacket, clears his throat until it's scratchy, while hissing, "I'm just tired of being flung from the hellhole of infinity…this is almost like *A Tale of Two Cities* or a Pandora's box or something!"

Dape gently touches the side of Michael's arm and says, "Now stop that, Michael. You're too far along to throw in the towel now! Do you really think that if you hadn't given up so much power to Alibabah when you were alive as Ishom that you would've had such issues with your self-esteem? You just can't throw in the towel when things get tough…it's not fair!"

She cups her hands to her chest, illustrating how like a mama bird, she needs to see if he's strong enough to fly before just pushing him out of the nest. If a person is strong, then he'll fly high into the sunlight. But if weak, he'll only come crashing to Earth's surface, defenseless. Trial and error simply breeds strength, and that's why he's had to go through these past life regressions.

Not really knowing what else to do right now, Michael shakes his head, yet things become a little bit clearer as Dape drops her hands to her sides, treating them like a balance scale, reminding Michael that if this mission is not fulfilled correctly, then there's a lifetime of suffering and sickness dead ahead. He looks at her and sees the elixir in her hand that can doubly delay his symptoms of HIV and tie him over until he reaches the holy room of Kullah. He already drank up the capsules she had sent him back to Earth with earlier, and he still needs to maintain speed, so he drinks up, downing the elixir to endure yet another showdown.

Noticing this silent form of an agreement, Dape claps her hands with glee as her aura shimmers with anticipation. She finishes up, telling Michael that she's got a little spot picked out on Earth, and he'll be goin' on a little tour! Yet Michael is instantly tipped-off by the lightheartedness of her angelic tone because he knows that nothing concerning Dape will ever be that easy. He politely asks her what the catch is as he takes a seat in the cushy chair, sitting upon the music sheets of time. She reaches in her go-pack and gives him a fresh towel and a glass of water just so he can get comfy. She then pulls out a gigantic universal calculator to see just how much time he has left on his journey. As she flips the calculator over to face him, it informs him that this is his last main stretch. The surrounding theatre has faded away, and he paces the floor composed of stars, wondering how he's gonna get all this done.

Given the fact that some elements of Earth have changed, there is no precise number she can really give him, but Dape pulls out a snow globe, which is representative of Earth's atmosphere, and he can see a thick white loop of smoke swirling throughout its zone. As he looks between his feet, the same type of vapor is rising up his legs, and it carries a distinct stench. Yet the original vaporized image hasn't been released from the snow globe. Actually, it appears that what happens within the glass dome later plays out beneath his feet in reality.

Dape then reaches below the table and pulls out a pin-striped box. She coughs a bit as the dust flies off of it, and upon opening it, the vacuuming effect of its magnetic pull sucks Michael inside its bottomless pit. Then Dape picks up the crystal ball and drops it into the enclosed fabric of space-time right behind him. Knowing what to expect, she pinches her nose, and then leans forward to be sucked into the terrestrial currents, which lead to Earth.

As the two dissolve from the protective, spiritual atmosphere and enter the plane of North America, they take on full flesh form, yet have entered into a separate time warp. It is present day of 2031, yet it doesn't look like the Earth he remembers. The two seem to be enclosed in an endless neighborhood of falling houses and playgrounds peppered with heroin needles. Meanwhile, common folks walk by wearing face masks.

Michael looks around, and angrily asks Dape what happened to his beloved home...ya know...the home of the brave where the kids in blue jean shorts play baseball on the evergreen blades of grass. It was the place where you could tear open a Good Humor bar without a swarm of flies devouring it before taking a second lick. She quickly pulls out a revised version of the declaration of independence, which is written in Spanish. While bundling up her Eskimo vest, she lets him know that back in his original past life as Jose, he had first managed to find a fraction of ancient Mexico's treasure, and then out of disappointment, he ordered a mass slaughter of the Mayans.

But the script of time was changed a bit during his past life regression. Jose was able to coax them into leading him to the sunken treasure, and they brought out tons of the most precious gold coins, engraved with kings and queens. By inheriting such wealth, Spain literally became invincible and was conquered by no other. Jose's actions changed history as we once knew it; therefore, the official language of the "states" is currently Spanish.

Upon the receipt of this information, Michael fastens the last button on his coat and is still flabbergasted at the fact that his hand managed to turn the wheels of time within such a short window, and he scratches his head in pure panic. Yet Dape lets him know that there's no time to get flustered right now. What he really should be doing is finding the way to Kullah to seize the correct anecdote. She hands Michael a leather-bound English-Spanish translator as a checkered cab slows down to pick them up. Dape also gives him a map to locate the anointed church that has the razor sharp steeple. His legs race rapidly to keep up with her, and she reaches over to hand Michael some cab fare, so he can pay the man with Spanish money. She's ready for the changed atmosphere on Earth, decked out in latex gloves, yet possessing all the spiritual knowledge she has, she doesn't bother to put on a mask like everyone else.

The media has sparked frenzy with the people via PSAs, which warn how HIV could now possibly be airborne. The average person on Earth wears a facemask to combat the virus, but it's not even airborne yet. With Dape's spiritual eye, she manages to see that the molecules of the virus do not possess enough elasticity to maintain a steady drift through Earth's oxygen levels. But they have evolved in the area of thickness and could possibly seep through a human being's pores to be transmitted through a common handshake.

So she explains to Michael that it is best to wear latex hand gloves. Upon explaining this new reality to him, she gives him a pair of his own and tells him to be safe and listen to his heightened intuition. Pay attention to the frequency levels of the mind, body and soul by tuning the ears and governing the true power of intention. This is the only way to reveal the key and prevent the plague from destroying the world. She takes one look at her precious jewel, and he gives off the vibe that he would like a companion for this journey. With puppy dog eyes, he silently pleads with her, and she tells him that if it's okay, then she would like to go along with him to the church to show him the true testament of a baptismal. He nervously nods while putting on his baseball cap as they get in the cab.

CHAPTER Sixteen

The Communion

As the taxi pulls up to the stony steeple's steps, Dape and Michael exit together. Fear has somehow been sucked from his bones as braveness reflects in his true aura. It covers every fear he once had about his untold future with the detail of certainty. They walk up the steps, taking in all the rainbow-colored, stained-glass windows, and the electric volts of excitement fuse from his palm as they hold hands. The currents then travel up his arm as he extends his other hand to open the church door. He looks at Dape, and she gives him the go-ahead. Meanwhile, a brush of something unknown flutters by his face. It's the mouth of hell! For the most part, he is protected from the dark elements as he enters the sacred building, while standing upon the middle ground of life. The church is a heavenly portal, but it is bound to Earth's surface, and Earth is Satan's playground. So upon entering the steeple, Michael will not be subject to a physical attack, but it is his soul that will be in limbo as he finishes the deed. They walk up to the crimson altar as Michael grabs the white railing to climb toward the small steps, which lead to the baptismal station. Dape pulls out her bible, the black beaded rosary, and a blue pill of existence. It's no bigger than a small Advil, but its potency unlocks the undiscovered stations of the mind to delay the responses of its synapses so one's mental machine is able to process such a large amount of energy + data and avoid the brink of insanity.

As Dape escorts him to the backroom so he can change into something more comfortable, she moves close to the side of the holy bath station and reads the prophetic prayer for a deeper level of exorcism. She needs to rid Michael's mind of the mental impurities that he has carried as a spiritual being for centuries and totally cleanse him so he can register with the same purity level of the hidden, sacred room of Kullah and seize the anecdote. As Dape makes the sign of the cross, Michael emerges from the backroom, dressed in black pants made of linen material, and he is shirtless. His sleek muscles bulge forth, and with his hair slicked back, he walks toward her with a sense of authority because it's time to take back what is his and enter the holy room. Dape lets him know how the pill of existence will first flush his mind, and upon nodding his head, he picks it up from the silver plate on the small table and smiles while grinding it with his teeth.

The water below is smoky and murky, and the steps, which descend into the baptismal, are white. But the water is so dark that the third step disappears as it is shallowly submerged beneath H2O. As he dips his right foot in the cool element, a soft chill flutters up the back of his leg, yet there is no turning back now. As Dape increases the strength of her prayer, which is layered with alliteration, her voice gathers with bass as she breaks into a light sweat due to the presence of the Holy Spirit.

As he then inches his way down, Michael's hips are now beneath the black waters and it feels like he's standing in an oversized ice chest. But as he lets go of the railing and falls back into the liquid matter, it begins to boil. The sudden shift in temperature would break any thermometer, yet his body is not impacted by the scorching elements. This is a case of mind over matter, and he appears to be winning against nature right now. Though the heat of the water has not damaged his exterior, its energy waves steadily seep through his pores, causing the potency of the pill to disintegrate and take effect at a rapid rate, separating his conscious mind from his body. And as he closes his damp eyes, his mind is now at a heightened state to control the universe, which is weathered with time.

His body remains still in the waters, but the projection of his soul is elevated toward the heavens as the runny film of iniquity rolls from his fingertips and toenails to be swallowed by the raging waters. As his soul rids itself from the bacteria associated with his karma from the lust of his past lives, along with murder, deception and lies, his body steadily jolts as electric shocks whip through his veins, reinforcing the sanctification of a purified mind.

Separated from the earth plane and completely wrapped within the mental universe of time, Michael's spirit starts to fall, travelling all the way down to the fiery nests of hell, where demons' jagged grins glow in the dark as they pound the captives' hands with a hammer and nails. Then Michael's mind travels a tad upward to another level, which is unnamed but has a sense of calm, and it is covered by the cool sediments that can be found in a summery rose garden.

Gathering the power of intention in his heart chakra, he determines that he must lead himself to the hidden room that has the healing anecdote. And by using his newfound mental electricity, he transmits mental waves throughout this milky atmosphere. On a scale of 10, the thrust of these waves registers at a 7, and can connect with the hidden portal of Kullah to capture the remedy. He speaks the command to launch his soul to this place, and right at the moment when his mind meshes with the correct frequency; his spirit is then transmitted to his desired destination, presently standing before a great, red door. And as he releases a pure sigh of relief, this red door that has a silver doorknocker and handle, gently unlocks itself as he speaks with authority, simply saying, "Command: Open."

At first the wonder of a wintry breeze blows right by him with sparkling snowflakes, yet as he progresses a little further down the hall, the temperature drastically changes. In universal time, if one goes only 2' ahead, then he can enter a new level of frequency and time zone as well. As a result of his body heat, the breezing snow melts away fast and Michael continues down an earthy cave to find a group of tiny, bronze-skinned, unsettled souls. These souls are holograms meant to lead him to the forsaken Mayans. They look like the same people he used to have bad dreams about as a child when he swore that the nightmares would steal his dreams. As a little boy, he didn't know what these people wanted, so he clinched his eyes shut…as tight as a bear trap…to block them out until daylight conquered the night.

When he was a boy, his apathetic appearance boggled the foreign spirits. Then confusion fueled into frustration and later anger. Hoping to capture Michael's attention, they used to moan all night in the corner of his room, and the next day he'd lay his head on his desk all day at school to try and soak in just one more ounce of precious sleep.

When that didn't work, the spirits became even more mischievous and started knocking over table lamps at night, gently scratching and rubbing his back, and pulling off his sheets repeatedly throughout the night. They didn't mean to be mean, but he was one of the very few people in the earth realm who had a spiritual eye that could see them, and they desperately needed his help!

Michael used to ask his grandmother to call the priest to perform an exorcism and get rid of these heathens, but his mother had overheard their conversation and quickly shut him up with the threat of a trip to the nuthouse. So Michael endured many years of torment alone, while fear sewed his mouth shut.

He slept with the lights on every night to watch out for the lurking demons, and fear seeped from his pores, but he never verbally responded to them. So after being ignored for such a long period of time, the voices just decided to stop all together.

Yet now, Michael can view these same people who are now locked within a designated section of the universe. The difference today is that he can apply his learned spiritual principles when dealing with them. Fear does not shake his bones anymore as he acknowledges the same entities that used to terrorize him as a child. Today, he's a full-grown man, and instead of turning to flee, he welcomes the people he was formerly fearful of to hear what they have to say. Being able to see them is proof that they were real all along. He wasn't crazy after all!

Pushing through the mildew of dormant fear, Michael has already honed the power of intention…and now the new key is to focus…focus on completing the mission.

Though these people are not composed of a physical, 3-D matter that is familiar within the earthly realm, they are still visible. Though one-dimensional in nature, they still have feelings and a heart. Powerful footsteps can be heard in the distance as the tribal leader emerges from the crowd. Ezonnie, who is the ruler of this time chain, stares Michael up and down and then extends his hand with a sense of pride.

Michael chuckles just a tad because the fear has completely dissolved from his psyche as he shakes his hand and engages this man in a calm, fluid conversation about the climate change, asking him how he manages to keep this whole place air-conditioned given how hot it is! The two men laugh in harmony as Ezonnie catches a genuine vibe from Michael, and he tells him that he knows what he's been waiting for.

Ezonnie leads the way, stomping toward the treasure chest with pride. He's a great man, king of the Mayans, the civilization anthropologists said was supposedly scattered and had practically disintegrated. He's around 6' 2", 270 pounds, and wears a headdress adorned by many symbols of human sacrifice. And even though it's obvious he possesses a great amount of strength, and could crush Michael with just one fist, the thought would never cross his mind. Peace is the only vibration that is permitted in this portal.

There is an unsaid air of respect between the two men as Michael and Ezonnie leave heavy footprints in the clay floor, and Ezonnie explains to him that the remedy is tucked away within the treasure chest. He enlightens Michael by telling him that his spiritual mission has been copied into the pages of existence since the day he was born. They've all been waiting for him to just make the first move toward his destiny! They stop and drop down in front of the wooden chest, which bears a sturdy iron lock, and the Mayan king first spins the combination to the number 2, then grinds it to 4, and finally stops at 43. This combination is composed of the exact date when the Spaniards first planned to conquer a large percentage of the Mayan population. This was the date when Michael first lived as Jose and had ordered a whirl of destruction to be cast upon the bronze people. In a way, this is Michael's chance to cancel out the karma that caused HIV. This is the only virus that had the ability to spread in such a rapid manner and kill multiple Spaniards who were later reincarnated across the globe. As a result, Michael was someone who was predestined for the bloody curse in light of his reign of terror as a Spanish captain.

But on February 4th, 1543, heaven chose to spare a group of favored people by designating them to reside inside this spiritual safety nest of Kullah, a magnetic layer of Earth's core, which is only visible from a spiritual standpoint. They were barricaded inside a treasure chest so they would never be harmed by human hands again.

And even though the entire world didn't wrong these people, the death toll accumulated by the Spanish soldiers had to be returned by massive means. So the Spanish karma began to manifest itself in the spiritual realm, and it took many years to decide how it should be returned.

But a little before the 1970s, a decision had been reached, and the Spaniards' spirits were sporadically returned to Earth by way of reincarnation, and they were programmed with a deadly generational curse to later take force in their veins, otherwise known as HIV.

Now you may be wondering how this could occur because not only Spanish people catch this virus; people all over the globe share its deadly mark. But when an individual's soul is reincarnated, the person can come back as any color, creed, or sex that the designer decides. And like Michael, their Spanish souls came back as people representative of every land across the world, and the curse later extended to their children.

Throughout the late '70s, early '80s, and with cross-cultural traveling, dating and marrying, the disease spread rapidly and flourished beyond control, serving as Satan's stepping stone to pummel existence. It works like this: In the spirit realm, Satan gets stronger with every soul he devours, and AIDS was a tool that the dark one created to slowly come into power. Think of it: If he is composed of millions of souls, then he becomes more powerful and can control and torture any of his subjects in the afterlife because he managed to kill them with something they helped him create through transferred karma. As Michael grabs the lock to make sure that the tick mark is securely set on the last number of 43, he intends to encounter the next step and end this evil spool of karma.

After the combo lock falls to the floor, the chest springs open in a ghostly fashion, radiating a golden, sparkling hue. Tucked inside are the true, tiny Mayan people who have been reduced to the size of toy soldiers to fit within the dimensions of the chest. The people Michael had first seen upon entry into Kullah were one-dimensional in nature, i.e., they were the back-up souls of the Mayans meant to ensure the tribe's survival.

But now he faces their original selves, the ones that were tucked away for safety. There seems to be a deep look of depression locked in all of their eyes. These people want to be free so badly and reunite with their lost family members, the ones who died and sat in purgatory during the wars with the Spaniards. They are the ones who refused to enter heaven without the company of their kin. But Michael now has the power to free them all, one-by-one, and it is significant that he personally frees the Mayans inside the chest because he was one of the key players responsible for unleashing such a severe amount of terror on their land. Michael takes this all in: the rusty combo lock, the weathered wooden trunk, and the people starving for love and affection. As a pure tear falls from Michael's eye and lands inside the chest, it only gives the Mayans a small amount of relief from its vaporizing effect. It soon evaporates as it hits the floor, which is as hot as flaming charcoal.

He wants to help them out, so he turns to Ezonnie for an answer, yet the tall, Mayan man just smiles, suggesting to him that all the answers must come from within.

Michael begins to replay the lessons in his head and remembers what happened to him in his very first past life regression. He possessed the power to empathize beyond human limitation when Dape cleared the irises of his eyes, which are the windows of the human soul. That's when he managed to occupy the body of that poor little Indian girl, and also intertwined with her emotions, while reliving her rape in the forest. He now wonders if that could cure the people's pain: To Empathize Beyond Limitation?

Now as he takes another look inside the chest, he just knows that he doesn't want to be in their situation and have to experience their levels of heated anguish, and he then wonders if there's another way to end their suffering.

Ezonnie bows his head and a charming breeze whips the temperature in the room to the crisp of cold. At the same time, hunched over, black-bellied trolls push at the sheer fabric that covers one side of the wall from top to bottom, which encloses the men within the sacred city of Kullah. These creatures are of a lower dimension; they are Satan's followers who are responding to the thickening amount of doubt that can be heard as it piles up in Michael's throat.

Eager to collect Michael, the final grand prize, they can see through the cream, stretchy curtain, and their nails start to shred through the delicate material. One creature's 3" claw completely punctures the veil, so Mike makes a split-second decision with the intention to reopen the irises of his eyes as he looks at the tiny, Mayan people to absorb their centuries of everlasting pain.

But it's not just one person that he's empathizing with this time; it's over 100 people who were spared as an exception, and they are all serving in the bigger picture of self-sacrifice that is intended to heal generations of anguish. This way, Michael can manifest the healing art of compassion and destroy the remnants of HIV by annihilating the negative karma he once racked up from his past life.

Yet the overload of misery and famine that Michael has decided to digest is flooding his vitals right now. His frame collapses from exhaustion as he throws his body across the chest, allowing hyper-electric volts to surge throughout his veins. This feels like 20 needle tips scraping across his dry skin. In order to bear the discomfort that comes with the transfer of pain, he gnashes his teeth, picking up the lock, squeezing it as tightly as a bottle of mustard. Meanwhile, the waterfall of compassion he has learned to generate steadily washes out the AIDS virus, which is deeply embedded within his own genetic pattern.

By the same token, the dark ones on the other side of the shaded curtain soon get swallowed whole by the oncoming fog and are chased away back to their former hiding places as the karma is destroyed by a person who had a hand in initiating it. Rapidly, Satan's plan is crumbling!

As the curse dries up within the cells of his spiritual flesh, Michael's frame of consciousness slowly drifts, detaching from the symphony of time. As the effects of the dream pill wear off, he clutches the sides of the chest tightly, while his spiritual body shakes as a delayed side effect as he continues to digest the drug. This is all simply a part of his mind meshing back with the garden of time, which is interwoven with the fabric of reality.

His soul takes a quantum leap through this zone that's almost like a subway portal, with tons of lights, as well as a flashing red hand that warns one to proceed with caution as the facial image of the devilish jaguar, Surai, disintegrates. There are various other mechanical devices along the way that assist a traveler on an expedient journey back through the ether. During this transmission, Michael's neon, spiritual self penetrates Earth's atmosphere again as his soul cocoons itself with his earthly body. And as he blinks his eyes open, he takes in the pitch black atmosphere around him. Upon gasping, he splashes through the skin of the baptismal water, while holding a heavy iron combo lock in-hand…a memento that he subconsciously pulled from the dream land.

He wipes his face off in awe as he stares at the rusty souvenir that he must have brought back from a distant time and place. He laughs with glee, wondering if this all could have really happened! As always, Dape is right there by his side with a glass of water and a warm towel. After he stumbles out of the water, he dries himself off a bit and tells her about all the things he just saw in another type of reality. She laughs, pinching his cheeks, informing him that he has just unfolded the secret world of reality. She picks the treasure map up from the front pew and lets him know that the bag full of gold at the end of the trail indicates that he won! He releases a cry of celebration, letting her know that he'd prefer to keep his feet firm on solid ground from now on if that's okay. She nods…letting him know that he did it...the storm is over now, and the thunder has subsided!

His ears perk up as if he didn't hear her correctly. She said that he did it...the karma is over? Does that mean that this is all over…including AIDS? As he bombards her with multiple questions, she simply reaches in her pocket and pulls out her phone, giving it to him so he can search the history of HIV for himself. As he types the abbreviation into Google, the Internet hourglass takes a whole minute until it stops spinning like a Ferris wheel and can find something related to the topic. Yet the only thing that comes up that is close to the term HIV is the DMV's brief description of an HOV lane, instructing the public that it is primarily meant for carpooling.

He covers his mouth, chuckling a bit, as the gentle heat from the new day radiates through the stained-glass window, gently drying out his linen pants. Dape says that she's gotta go for now, but reminds him that she is very proud of him. She cheers, "You did it, my boy! You destroyed the plague and devoured the hidden karma. You are officially awesomeness!"

After kissing his cheek and hugging him close, she flings her hair while putting on her sunglasses. And as she takes off her coat and proceeds to exit through the double doors to the fresh, crisp air outside, Michael begs her to wait a minute as he slips on a white T-shirt. They need to take pictures together! He wants to know some more about what she likes to do in her free time…he still has questions he'd like to ask…spiritual questions that she may be able to clarify for him. He asks her where she's from. He just wants to know more about the lady who in a way saved his life! She kindly asks him to take a picture of her with the cell phone, and the two cuddle up for a warm snapshot. And as he pushes the little, white button down and the flash goes off, he takes a photo of a very special woman.

To the naked eye, she's just an average, cute girl. But right before she's about to go, she hands him a clear phone cover and asks him to place it on top of the device to see a secret in 3-D. He seems confused, but desperate to know more about the lady he's been hanging out with all this time, he follows her instructions and clips the cover in place as shades of Technicolor ripple across the screen with vast clarity. While tilting the phone against the reflection from the church's stained-glass windows, a new image of her facial silhouette comes into focus. Her beautiful features gain depth, tying the lady's true identity to that of Michael's mother, who had passed away from the virus years ago! Tears drip down his face as his voice box mutes itself with shock.

He is overwhelmed with inexplicable emotions right now, and although she took on a slightly different appearance as she came to him as Dape, the decoding case cover definitely identifies the woman he knows all too well. This was his mother, in full disguise, who used to tuck him in and recite the Lord's Prayer with him as a child. With this news, he races down the red, suede aisle and although he couldn't be more than 15 feet from the exit, he feels like he's stuck on a never-ending, reversed escalator that separates him from the woman he desperately loves.

By the time he manages to make it outside, she has faded into the crowd. He steps out in the midst of the people to see if he can spot her likeness anywhere, but all he sees are people who haven't even bothered to put on face masks to avoid HIV because in this new twist of reality, no one has ever heard of such a thing.

The plague of the past just got wedged into a separate time warp within the universal clocks. Since the deal is totally sealed now, Michael knows that his health is in good standing. But does this hold true for his mother as well? What will happen to her since she had already passed due to the virus? He begins to have outlandish thoughts, wondering if it's even possible that she could be given a second chance at life since she had died from a curse that no one seems to know of anymore. The sheer thought of its perplexity is too much to take right now, but he desperately wants to find her to know if there's any way he can help. He fervently paces the sidewalk, showing multiple people the phone pic he just took of her, both with and without the case cover. As he anxiously attempts to locate his mother, the passing people shrug their shoulders in a blank response, indicating that they've never seen her before. Combing his fingers through his jet-black hair, he tucks the phone away inside his pant pocket. Yet to his surprise, there's an envelope inside, and it holds the title and key to his new record label as was promised. The thought of grasping his dream in the music industry once mesmerized him, but his newly found self wonders how great it would really be without sharing it with his mother.

His friend, Dale, gives him a call and as Michael asks him if he still needs a blood transfusion, Dale laughs because he doesn't even remember the car accident. In this stretch of reality, it's as if the tragedies of the past never took place.

Meanwhile, a newspaper blows down the freshly swept sidewalk and clings to Michael's pant leg, and he picks it up to read about the new world. Yet he can't help but notice that it's written in English. Spanish is no longer the dominant language in the US. The correct order of everything appears to have been restored to its pleasant and peaceful state, and as Michael pulls the moist combination lock from his other pocket, he clamps it closed, signifying that the victory is won! And as Dale tells him about the big football game last night, Mike can't help but wonder about the whereabouts of his mother. He once felt that the true joy of life would come after he discovered the karma that had created AIDS. But with newfound health, he's curious if the richness of reality could become even sweeter if he could manage to turn its pages with the lady who gave him his very first breath of life.